Praise for Bill Pronzini's *Dead Run*

"For a combination of adventure, mystery and straight
action, *Dead Run* will be hard to beat. . . . Here
Pronzini has retained his basic locale and central
character used so successfully in *The Jade Figurine*. . . .
There is a bang-up finale. . . . *Dead Run* is a lot of
fun to read, it is well written and it has a rakish
adventurer with whom we all can identify."
—*The New York Times*

"Stylish writing, an exotic locale and deft character-
ization add up to a treat. . . . Shocks follow surprises
as the story rushes on and arrives at a throat-clutching
climax." —*Publishers Weekly*

Other *Mystery Scene* books available from
Carroll & Graf:

*Beyond the Grave*
by Marcia Muller and Bill Pronzini

*Buyer Beware*
by John Lutz

*The Jade Figurine*
by Bill Pronzini

*Tough Tender*
by Max Allan Collins

# Dead Run

# BILL PRONZINI

Carroll & Graf Publishers, Inc.
New York

Published by arrangement with the author.

Originally published by The Bobbs-Merrill Company, Inc.

First Carroll & Graf edition 1992

Carroll & Graf Publishers, Inc.
260 Fifth Avenue
New York, NY 10001

ISBN: 0-88184-838-7

Manufactured in the United States of America

For CYLVIA and LEO MARGULIES —

*Two of the Nicest People Anywhere*

# Dead Run

# 1

The name of the boat on which I booked passage from Singapore was the S.S. *Pangkor*, and she was one of the last single-stack steamers that carried passengers and minor cargoes to and from the smaller port towns scattered along both coasts of the Malay Peninsula. Transportation facilities in this part of Southeast Asia have improved vastly over the past twenty years—on land, on sea, and in the air—and there are half a dozen faster, more convenient ways to travel or ship merchandise; but the steamers operate on a shoestring, and people without much money or with a frugal or nostalgic nature use them enough to keep them operating. You get occasional adventuresome tourists, but for the most part the passenger lists are made up of poor native laborers, tired drifters and expatriates from a score of different countries, owners and employees of the tiny three- to five-acre rubber plantations known as smallholdings, and a mixture of minor businessmen, gamblers, shopkeepers, and whores.

The *Pangkor* was an ancient craft—the deck boarding creaked every time you took a step and her white paint had peeled and faded so that she had a tawdry, patchwork-gray look about her—but the cabins were spacious and clean, if you could afford a cabin, and the food was usually good and the liquor prices reasonable. In most ways I liked her far more than I could ever like one of the modern tourist boats that plied both the Strait of Malacca and the South China Sea. She may have been old and frowsy, but she had charm, and she was part of an exotic old world which was rapidly being swallowed by a less appealing, sterilized new one.

Her run was the west coast, from Singapore Island below the southernmost tip of the Peninsula to Langkawi Island at the northernmost tip. She stopped in places like Batu Pahat and Malacca and Port Dickson and Port Swettenham, among others; but I was only going as far as the last, some 200 nautical miles from Singapore. Once I got there I would disembark and take a bus another twenty-odd statute miles to Kuala Lumpur. And in K.L., Martin Quayles would supply a car that would bring me to his rubber estate forty additional miles away, in the lower belly of Selangor's rubber country.

Quayles's estate was fairly large at 300 acres, and it was called the Union Jack. The British used to control three-quarters of the Malayan rubber industry, primarily through agency houses, but in recent years more and more Chinese have taken over the larger commercial plantations. Men like Quayles, however, who have been dealing in rubber for decades, hang onto their holdings tenaciously. He had a couple of replanted *kaboons* that had been unproductive for seven years and which were now ready to yield again, and he needed a man to supervise the Malay work force on those acreages. Overseers aren't that easy to find these days—the pay isn't much and you're usually stuck out in the middle of nowhere—and he had been having trouble locating someone with experience in rubber.

When I heard about this, from the head of a small agency house, I had decided to contact Quayles. I've lived in Singapore since the middle sixties, and especially in the past three years it has become more of a home to me than any other place in the world. But decent work is scarce there, and the tourists have begun to overrun the island, and the guiding hand of Prime Minister Lee Kuan Yew has turned to iron. In recent months the Singapore Parliament had passed a number of radical laws, among them ones providing for hanging or caning and life imprisonment for those convicted of or complicity in armed robbery and gun-running; beating and lengthy prison terms for traffickers in illegal immigrants; jailing or fining and deportation of known criminals. Statutes like these were supposed to protect public welfare, and in that respect they were conceivably valid enough. But the latter made life potentially harsh for a man with my past—and there were other laws and practices which I disliked and disagreed with, such as a ban on smoking in a variety of public places, the harassment and jailing of kids with long hair and "improper" clothing, the too-righteous railing against "moral and material pollution." I still felt deep personal ties with Singapore, and I knew I would want to come back to her someday—but right now I needed and wanted a change.

So I had telephoned Quayles at his estate and told him frankly that while I had worked rubber before, it had been for only a brief period; but, I said, I was certain I could handle the job and would even be willing to accept a lower salary than I had been told he was offering. He'd said he would think it over, and a week later I received a letter saying that he had decided to put me on on a conditional basis and instructing me to be in K.L. seven days hence.

3

I gave up my flat in Punyang Street, in Singapore's Chinatown, and packed my few belongings into a large rattan suitcase. I had been working steadily if not too profitably for an Englishman named Harry Rutledge, who owned a waterfront godown, and I had sufficient funds for cabin passage on the *Pangkor*, with more than enough left over to buy a new bush jacket and jungle boots and some other items I would need in Selangor. I did each of those things the day of departure, a hot, windless Saturday in early October. I also made a courtesy call, before setting out to board the steamer, on Inspector Kok Chin Tiong of the Singapore police; a year ago, when old bitch Fate had dragged me into a complicated and near-fatal mess involving the theft of a priceless jade figurine from the Museum of Oriental Art, Tiong had first hassled me and then, surprisingly, done an unprecedented about-face and more or less saved me from official reprisal. But there were no friends to say good-bye to, male or female; no ties of any kind to sever. Being alone in the world—alone by choice—has its advantages at times.

The *Pangkor* steamed out of Singapore Harbor at 4 P.M. I had found my cabin immediately after boarding, put my suitcase on one of its two bunks, and then had come out on deck again. I stood at the starboard cabin deck rail with several other passengers, taking my last look for an indeterminate period at the Lion City's rust-colored tile roofs.

One of those other passengers was a tall, fleshy, sable-haired girl in her late twenties—Filipina, I thought. Her nose was too small, her mouth too wide, and she wore far too much makeup; but high round breasts and a fine body and huge black hungry eyes combined to give her an aura of sensuality that drew and held my attention. I caught her eye and smiled at her, but she wasn't having any. An elderly planter type in a crisp tropical suit tried his luck a couple of minutes later, and she appraised him and then put on a broad smile; they began a conversation which I could not help but overhear. She told him in broken English that her name was Maria Velasquez, and that she was on her way to Kuala Lumpur, and he said his name was Phelps or Phillips and invited her to have a drink with him. They went into the ship's saloon, and I stood there and allowed myself a small wry smile. I looked like what I was and Phelps or Phillips looked like what he was: simple as that. Nobody gives anything away in Southeast Asia these days, and nobody sells anything cheap when they can sell it dear, particularly on a tired old lady like the *Pangkor*.

I stayed on deck until we had passed through the outer corner of Keppel Harbor and into the Strait of Malacca. Then I decided I could use something for the heat, too, and entered the saloon. It was a large room, noisy and crowded, but there were stools free at the bar. I sat on one of them, ordered an iced Anchor beer from the white-singleted barman. The planter type and Maria Velasquez had their heads together at a corner table. She was laughing at everything he said and rubbing one of her breasts against his arm; she seemed to have him hooked, all right, and it would cost him plenty before she let him do anything about it. Better you than me after all, brother, I thought.

There were dishes of katchung seeds on the bar, and I nibbled on those and drank my beer and looked out through the starboard windows at the passing greenery of Pulau Kukup, the small island off the tip of Johore. I'd been doing that for ten minutes when the youngish man in the rumpled white suit came in and sat down next to me. He had heavy pouches under his eyes, as if he hadn't slept for some time. His hair was red and unkempt, and his beard-stubbled face looked parboiled; he was either a recent arrival in Southeast Asia, or he had the kind of skin which didn't tan no matter how much exposure it had. When he ordered a plain arrack, one of the worst things you can drink in the heat, his accent told me he was British.

Waiting, he got out a handkerchief and worked it over his face. I saw that his hand seemed to be shaking slightly. The barman brought his arrack, and the hand shook more noticeably as he raised the glass. Alcoholic, I thought—but the drink didn't seem to do anything to settle him down. He fumbled in his coat pocket and brought out a package of Australian cigarettes and got one of them into his mouth, but then he couldn't seem to find a light.

I said, "Here you go," and slid my box of wax matches across the bar to him.

His eyes flicked over me, went to the matches, came back to me again. "Oh I say, thank you, very kind of you." He got the cigarette going and pushed the box back to me, exhaling smoke through both mouth and nostrils. Then he used the handkerchief on his flushed cheeks again. "Beastly hot, isn't it?"

"As usual."

"I don't care at all for this part of the world; can't think why I should ever have come out. I shall return home shortly, though—quite soon, yes. To London. Kensington. It's a lovely city, London. Have you ever been?"

"No."

"Lovely city."

"Sure," I said.

"My name is Kirby, Richard Kirby."

He seemed to find relief for his nervousness in conversation. I had nothing better to do, so I decided to indulge him—for a while, anyway. "I'm Dan Connell," I told him.

"You're an American, aren't you?" He didn't wait for an answer. "I'm British, of course. Used to be with Barclays in Kuala Lumpur, transferred from London eighteen months ago. Lost my position in August. Bloody officials discovered I

6

had a penchant for fan-tan, all very innocent, and determined I was no longer trustworthy. I was with them eleven years, not a blemish on my record, and of a sudden I'm no longer trustworthy. Filthy bureaucrats. Went to Singapore to look for a new position, but had no luck at all. Should have known it would be that way, really."

"Things'll work out," I said. "They usually do."

"Yes. Soon, quite soon." He jabbed out his cigarette and immediately lit another with one of my matches. "Bloody officials, all their bloody fault."

"How's that?"

"If they hadn't sacked me, I should never have—" Kirby broke off abruptly and gave me a half-frightened look, as if he thought that maybe he was starting to talk too much. He finished his arrack, got off his stool and put two Malaysian dollars on the bar. "Well," he said to a spot a couple of inches to my left, "I should be off for some fresh air. Nice chatting with you, Mr. Conners."

"Sure," I said. "Same here, Mr. Kimbly."

He didn't seem to hear that; turning, he walked rapidly out of the saloon. He was a strange one, all right. But then, Southeast Asia is a mecca for strange types.

All God's chillun got problems, I thought—and ordered another round.

# 2

I ate an early supper in the small dining room: *ohtak ohtak*, which is normally a Malay delicacy—prawns soaked in coconut milk and spices and baked in coconut leaves—but which turned out to be something a bit less in the hands of the *Pangkor's* galley staff. It was just dusk when I went out on deck again.

On most days in this part of the world, twilight is very short; but sometimes it lingers a bit longer and the sky is tinged with an odd yellowish afterglow—what the Malays call *mambang kuning*. The western horizon was suffused with it tonight, and it had the ugly jaundiced appearance of thick smog. Looking at it, you could almost believe the old native Malay superstition that it portends the activity of evil spirits.

Below it, a mass of jungle encroaching on the waterline rose like a high, unbroken wall. Even out here on the Strait you could smell its dank, decaying odor; within the tangled vegetation, it would be overpowering. The rain forests of Malaysia are some of the most primeval anywhere, steaming hot and damp and oppressive, filled with leeches and snakes and bats and tigers and a thousand other things. They're a damned fine place to stay out of.

I watched the *mambang kuning* fade into a kind of rich purple-black color. A handful of scattered stars began to shine like gemstones, and the ship's lights and a fat tropical moon put a luminescent gold sheen on the smooth dark water. To the north, lights appeared along the shore, and the steamer altered her course and began to move toward them: Batu Pahat, our first stop.

When the *Pangkor* came into Batu Pahat's small harbor, I walked forward and stood idly with a knot of passengers who were waiting to disembark. A launch came out, and a small cargo lighter; floodlamps illuminated both craft as they drew up alongside. Two men, both Caucasians, got off the launch and stood on the gangway float, studying each of the departing passengers as they came down. They were dressed casually in white pongee jackets and slacks—one very tall and very thin, the other short and squat with an upper lip adorned by a thick, squarish mustache. Mutt and Jeff.

They waited until all the passengers had boarded the launch, and then they came up the gangway and paused on deck and looked around. Their eyes touched me, lingered briefly, moved away. Mutt said something to Jeff, and they came aft past me and entered the saloon.

The passenger launch started back to Batu Pahat, red and green running lights winking like colored *kelip-kelip* in the darkness. The cargo lighter was taking on several small boxes and crates from the *Pangkor's* lower storage deck, and I could hear the Malay crewmen chattering as they worked. I lit a cigarette and dropped the match over the rail.

Someone behind me said, "Pardon."

I turned, and it was Mutt—the short one with the mustache. There was no sign of Jeff. He gave me a smile with a gold tooth in one corner of it. "I'm looking for a friend of mine," he said, "an Englishman named Kerwin. He apparently boarded in Singapore. Red-haired fellow, ruddy-faced, possibly wearing a wrinkled white suit. Would you happen to have seen him?"

Mutt's speech was faintly accented, but I couldn't place its origin; his English, though, contained more of an American than a British flavor. He had oddly shaped eyes that would start to blink and not quite make it, so that he seemed to be half-squinting from time to time. I didn't particularly like those eyes, or his gold-toothed smile.

I said, "Sorry, no."

He dipped his head sideways, in a kind of parrotlike movement, and turned abruptly and walked up to the bow and disappeared into the amidships passageway. Another peculiar type, I thought—damned peculiar. Well, friend of the Englishman's or not, he'd find him sooner or later; the *Pangkor* wasn't all that large a boat. As the Malays say, *Tida apa*. Less polite American translation: the hell with it.

When the cargo lighter had finished loading, and we were on our way again, I went to my cabin. It was like an oven in there; the ancient punkah on one bulkhead did nothing for the circulation of air. I opened the porthole a little, took from my suitcase my small leather carry-all in which I had toilet articles and cigarettes and a slender cash reserve and the letter I'd received from Martin Quayles, and brought it into the head. Then I showered in the tiny stall and shaved and rubbed skin ointment onto the perpetually heat-burned area across the back of my neck.

Stretched out naked on one of the bunks, I listened to the sibilant hiss of the bow cutting through small swells and to occasional screeches from the scavenger seabirds that come out to reconnoiter passing ships, looking for discharges of garbage. I dozed after a while, but it was too hot to fall into a comfortable sleep. There were half a dozen mosquito bites on my arms and legs when I woke—we were still in close to

10

shore—and I stood to close the porthole. That made the cabin all the more stifling again. My throat was dry, and I decided I'd go to the saloon for an iced beer and sit in there until it either grew cooler or I got tired enough to sleep in spite of the heat. I put on a clean bush jacket, a pair of khakis, and went to the door and opened it.

Kirby was standing there, right hand upraised in a knocking position and left hand wrapped around a three-quarters-full bottle of arrack.

He jumped half a foot, almost dropped the bottle, recovered in time, and put on a smile that trembled and fell away almost instantly. He was sweating, and he looked to be twice as nervous as he had been earlier.

"Hullo," he said. "You gave me a start. May I come in?"

"I was just going to the saloon."

"I've arrack here, Conners, we'll have some of that. Why pay for a toddy when you can have it free? Yes."

I started to tell him that I didn't drink anything but beer, but he pushed past me and sat himself down on the bunk I was using for a luggage rack. He put the bottle of arrack on the bulkhead shelf between the bunks. I closed the door and came over and looked at him.

"How did you know my cabin?" I asked.

"Saw you entering before we left Singapore." He had the cap off the bottle. "I say, have you any glasses?"

"There are a couple in the head."

"Yes, of course."

Kirby got up and went in there. I heard water splash into the cracked porcelain basin. When he came out again a couple of minutes later, his face and hair were damp and he was carrying the two tumblers. He sat again and poured arrack into each of them; picked up his and put it off neat and poured a second.

I said, "Your two friends find you, did they, Kirby? Or is it Kerwin?"

His head jerked. "What are you talking about? I don't know what you mean."

He knew what I meant, all right. His eyes had bright fear in them. "They got on at Batu Pahat," I said. "One of them asked me about you."

"What . . . did you tell him?"

"Nothing. Look, Kirby, if you're in trouble I don't want any part of it."

"I'm not in trouble. Certainly not." He laughed, but so falsely it did nothing except underscore the fact that he was lying.

"No? Well, why did you come here?"

"Simply wanted some company. Hate to drink alone."

"If you're trying to hide from those two men, you're plain out of luck. I don't suppose they're police—they didn't act like police—but it doesn't really matter. I'm sure as hell not going to let you sleep in here tonight, and anyway you can't stay on board indefinitely."

Kirby drained his second arrack and reached for the bottle again.

I said, "I don't want you getting drunk in here, either."

He stood up, clutching the arrack bottle by the neck. "You're quite an understanding person, aren't you, Connell? Quite sympathetic."

"Oh Christ," I said. "Listen, I've had enough grief to last me the rest of my life and I'm not about to invite any more. I'm just not going to get mixed up in your problems or anybody else's. If that makes me a bastard, then I'm a bastard and the hell with it. Good-bye, Kirby—I wish you luck."

He started to say something, changed his mind, and went out without looking at me again. The door banged shut loudly behind him.

I went over and opened the porthole again, because the

sour odor of Kirby's sweat hung heavily on the stale air. I wanted a beer more than ever now. So I shut off the bulkhead lamp and left the cabin immediately, locking the door after me, and found my way to the saloon.

It was still crowded and still noisy. I didn't see Mutt and Jeff, or Kirby, or for that matter Maria Velasquez and the elderly planter type. There were half a dozen card games in progress—*pai-gow* and bridge—and since people were jammed two deep at the bar, I stood kibitzing one of the bridge games once I had managed to buy a bottle of Anchor. It featured an interesting cosmopolitan match-up: two Australians against a Chinese and a Malay. I don't particularly care for bridge, but these four were playing for money and with a vengeance. Orientals lose their well-publicized inscrutability when it comes to gambling; they seem to approach any game of chance with an almost hysterical fanaticism. And Asians tend to display the same emotional involvement. The Chinese and the Malay made a colorful team, and a vocal one in three languages. But the Australians had superior skill, and it looked to me as though the stakes would be in their pockets at the end of the final rubber.

Along with several others I watched the game for more than an hour. During that time the planter type, Phelps or Phillips, put in an appearance—alone and looking disgruntled. I wondered perversely if the Filipina had demanded for her favors, as they used to say, more money than he was willing to put out. Well, it was none of my business. But looking at him off by himself, seeing him drink stengahs with a kind of grim steadiness, I couldn't help but feel a little sorry for him.

My prediction as to the outcome of the bridge match proved accurate: the Aussies won, though not by much. The saloon crowd began to thin rapidly once it was over, and pretty soon there were no more than half a dozen people left, including Phillips or Phelps; it was near midnight by then. I had one last beer as a nightcap and drifted out on deck.

The starboard rail was deserted. I moved aft, lighting my last cigarette with my last match. Some of the thick heat was gone now; a light wind had come up and the air was tinged with the smell of rain, freshening it considerably. Out on the Straits behind us I could see the close-spaced running lights of what was probably a nightfisher. Shoreward a fan of illumination tinted the horizon—Malacca Town, a half hour or so away—and above that dark masses of clouds had begun to obscure the bright face of the moon. We were in for a tropical storm in another couple of hours.

I stopped near the end of the superstructure. It was very still, except for muted voices on the main deck below and, once, a single blast of the *Pangkor's* whistle. I leaned on the rail, smoking and looking down at the black water.

And that was when the woman screamed.

# 3

It was a brief, sharp cry that came from around the corner of the superstructure, and it was followed immediately by the distant splashing sound of something hitting the water off the stern. I ran back there, swinging around a row of folded siesta chairs. The woman who had screamed was thirty feet away, turned toward me and just starting to run. Behind her, rushing hard away from the taffrail, were two men—one short and one very tall. Even in the darkness I recognized all three instantly: Maria Velasquez, and Mutt and Jeff.

I'd taken two strides toward the Filipina when Jeff caught her shoulder in a long reach and spun her around toward him. She screamed again, low in her throat, and he hit her across the side of the head with a brutal, sweeping forearm. She flew to one side, slid jarringly to her knees, and then collapsed in a crumpled heap. Anger flared inside me, and I thought, *You son of a bitch!* and went after him.

When I got to where he was I had my right arm locked into a horizontal bar, fingers stiff and extended; but he'd had just enough time to set himself, and the instant I jabbed at his breastbone he sidestepped with swift agility. My fingers ripped across the front of his pongee jacket, leaving me off-balance and exposed. He slammed that forearm against my ribs, and it was like being hit with something made of iron. Pain burst upward through my chest, took my breath away. I reeled toward the other one. Mutt kicked at my ankles, connected glancingly, and I went down hard on my buttocks. Open-mouthed, gasping, I saw him swing the foot again. I twisted my head away from it, grabbed for it as it shot upward, caught the material of his trousers and then the soft flesh of his calf, and heaved straight up. He went into the air like a man starting a backflip, landed bellowing on his shoulders and nearly tripped Jeff lunging in behind him.

I rolled twice, rapidly, across the creosoted deck to starboard, and heard as I did so voices raised distantly amidships, the staccato slap of running footsteps. When I came up against the bulwark I could see Jeff stopped several paces away, head swiveled toward the approaching sounds. Behind him, Mutt struggled to his feet and shouted something I didn't quite catch and then ran toward the port rail. Jeff hesitated, looking at me, at the prostrate girl; then he pivoted abruptly after Mutt. I used the railing to heave myself up just as three Chinese came pounding out onto the stern. I shoved past them, pain burning in my ribs and the one ankle, and limped to port; but by the time I got to where I could see around the superstructure both Mutt and Jeff were gone.

The Chinese were standing over the girl, chattering in Canton dialect, when I came back. She had begun to stir, moaning faintly. I knelt beside her, still trying to breathe normally, and got a hand under her head and lifted it. Her eyes fluttered open, glazed at first but then widening in a fresh wash of terror. Her body tensed and I thought she was going to scream again; I said quickly, "It's all right, they're gone, it's all right." It took a moment, but finally her body relaxed and a dull film of pain replaced the fear in her eyes. She made a whimpering sound, said something I didn't understand in what was probably Tagalog.

One of the Chinese helped me get her onto her feet. I put an arm around her and braced her body with my own. The one who had helped me spoke in Cantonese; I shook my head and asked him if he knew English, and that got me a head shake in return. I made a gesture with my left hand, to indicate that matters were under control, and then I walked the girl away across the stern. I heard them begin talking again, excitedly, as we entered the cabin passageway, but they didn't follow.

When I got her to my cabin, I unlocked the door and took her inside and sat her down on one of the bunks. Then I put on the bulkhead lamp and locked the door again. She sat there with her head down, hands clasped under her breasts. A blackening welt discolored her right temple where Jeff had clubbed her, and there was a tear in her skirt and dark creosote stains on both the skirt and her sweater.

I went into the head and ran water over a facecloth and brought it out to her. She held it gingerly against her temple, said softly, "Thank you."

"What happened out there, Maria?"

"You know my name?"

"I heard you talking out on deck before we left Singapore," I said. "Now what happened? Why did you scream?"

"Those men . . . I see them throw another man into the water. I am coming out and I see them do that."

I remembered the splash I'd heard. "What man?"

"I do not know. A man in a white suit."

Kirby, all right, I thought. "Was he alive?"

"I do not know."

"Well, did he fight them?"

"I think no, but it happen so quick . . ."

17

"Okay, just take it easy." I reached out to the shelf, picked up the glass of arrack Kirby had poured for me but that I hadn't touched, and handed it to her. "Try a little of this."

She drank, coughed, drank again. Color came into her cheeks. "You have a cigarette, *Ginoong*, yes?"

I got a fresh pack and a box of matches from my carry-all, and lighted a cigarette for her. She exhaled smoke in a sporadic stream. Her hands still trembled, and the dark eyes clung to my face.

"If those men they find me now," she said, "they will throw me into the water too . . ."

"Nobody is going to throw you into the water," I said. "We'll go up and tell the captain what happened, and he'll find those two and put them under ship's arrest."

"But no! Then there will be police when we reach Malacca. I do not wish trouble with the police, I do not wish anything to do with the police."

There was new fright in her voice, and I thought that she'd probably had a brush or two with the authorities in the past. Which gave us something of a common history, as well as a common purpose of noninvolvement. Still, my conscience wouldn't allow me to ignore what had just happened. The Straits are full of sharks and Kirby had likely been either dead or unconscious when they'd pitched him over; but there was still a chance, however slim, that he was alive and could be rescued. And I didn't care at all for the idea of a pair like Mutt and Jeff running around free to beat up on women and kill people when they felt like it.

I said, "The captain's got to be told, Maria. For your own protection, as much as anything else."

"Then you go to him alone, yes? Do not tell him about me."

"Suppose those three Chinese already got word to him?"

"Please," she said. "Please, *Ginoong*."

I sighed softly. "Yeah—all right."

She gave me a look of nervous relief. "I can stay here until you are coming back?"

"It's probably the safest place for you," I agreed. I went to the door. "Lock it as soon as I leave, and don't open it for anyone but me."

"Yes. I will do that."

In the passageway I waited until I heard the lock click on the inside; then I went forward and up onto the bridge. We were coming into Malacca now. Off the starboard bow I could see harbor lights, and the lights of the town spread out in a bright sweep behind it—maybe five minutes away. The sky was heavily overcast to the north, and the faint rumbling of thunder came from that direction. The wind had gotten stronger, carrying moisture that touched my face like mist.

When I entered the semidarkened pilothouse, the thin, sixtyish man in captain's braid turned from the wheel and asked irritably, in German-accented English, what I was doing there. I told him—all of it, except for Maria Velasquez. The three Chinese hadn't reported the fight and so he was doubtful at first; but the condition of my clothing, and the fresh bruises I showed him on my ankle and along my ribcage, convinced him I was in sober earnest. It was too late for him to turn the *Pangkor* around, he said then—by that time we'd already come past the breakwater, into Malacca harbor—but he ordered the radio operator to contact the port authorities; they'd send out a search boat. I made a close guess as to how long it had been since Kirby was tossed over, and the captain fixed an approximate position on his charts and relayed that information through the radioman. Then he told the first officer, a mild-eyed Malay, to instigate a search of the ship as well as to delegate members of the crew to watch for any men answering my description of Mutt and Jeff who might attempt disembarking on the Malacca shuttle launch.

After the first officer had gone, the captain, whose name

was Holzmein, instructed me to wait there with him until Mutt and Jeff had been taken into ship's custody. I had expected that, and I nodded and went over to the starboard windows. From there I could see down to the lighted gangway on the main deck, where half a dozen passengers and four crewmen waited at the rail. If there was going to be any action in that vicinity, I had a box seat for it.

Halfway across the harbor Holzmein ordered the engines shut off and the anchor dropped. As soon as that was done two boats came out from the docks, one of them the launch and the other a larger, newer craft that looked to be a patrol boat. That one angled past us to port, heading out into the Strait, while the launch drew up to the float at the foot of the gangway. I watched two of the crewmen carry down sacks of mail, followed by the handful of disembarking passengers. There didn't seem to be any cargo for offloading, probably because Malacca was a fairly good-sized port and a number of coast-run freighters stopped there regularly.

I lit a cigarette. It didn't look as though Mutt and Jeff had gotten it in their heads to try the launch, and that was no doubt because they'd anticipated my reporting what had happened. The *Pangkor* wasn't large enough to offer any hiding places which might be overlooked in a general search, and if they realized that—and decided not to try remaining on board anyway and maybe running a bluff of innocence— they had only one alternative: to get off the steamer by some means other than the launch. And if they'd acted quickly after the fight, they had had enough time to do just that. . . .

It was what the bastards *had* done, all right; the first officer confirmed it when he returned hurriedly to the pilothouse less than two minutes later.

A passenger strolling on the lower storage deck had seen the two of them slip over the side as soon as the *Pangkor* cut power, and swim away in the darkness. The first officer had put a spotlight on the harbor water immediately, but to no avail.

Holzmein notified the port authorities, who in turn notified the regular police—and that took it out of the captain's hands entirely and my sphere of influence at least momentarily. There was some debate as to whether or not I should be asked to come ashore, to tell my story firsthand and make a formal statement and identify Mutt and Jeff if and when they were apprehended. But finally they determined that that would be unnecessary at the moment, and instead told Holzmein to hold the *Pangkor* there in the harbor while they awaited developments.

So I stood around the pilothouse, mostly silent, and half an hour passed before we had further word from shore. The first report that came over the radio was that they hadn't found Mutt and Jeff on shore, or anyone who had seen them. The second report was from the patrol boat which had gone out looking for Kirby. They had searched the area, and hailed the nightfisher I'd seen earlier; he hadn't been found either. I would have been surprised if he had been. Whatever the poor clown had been mixed up in, it had earned him a watery grave at best and turned him into a meal for the sharks at worst. I felt a small sense of guilt for not having let him hide in my cabin, but then I thought Mutt and Jeff would probably have gotten him anyway, sooner or later, and that I had acted reasonably and advisedly. Empathy is a fine human emotion, but when you're already carrying a heavy burden yourself you just don't have room for the ones carried by strangers.

The Malacca authorities did not locate Mutt and Jeff in the next half hour, and reached the conclusion that it wouldn't be necessary at all for me to come ashore. They took my name and point of disembarkation and an address where I could be reached—the Union Jack—and then said both the *Pangkor* and I were free to continue up the coast.

21

Which was a considerable relief; I had no desire for a session of any kind with the local constabulary.

Once we'd gotten underway again, I told Holzmein which cabin I was in and then went down off the bridge and into the cabin passageway. When I knocked on my door, there was no response. Frowning, I knocked again. Still nothing. I reached out and turned the latch handle—and the door swung open under my hand, revealing muggy darkness. I leaned in and switched on the bulkhead lamp.

Maria Velasquez was gone.

Nothing that I could see had been disturbed; and with her locked in it didn't figure Mutt and Jeff could have found out where she was and gotten to her before their escape over the side. So she had to have left voluntarily—either because she'd grown tired of waiting, which was possible but not probable in view of the circumstances, or because she had come to the impulsive decision that leaving the *Pangkor* entirely was the way to insure her safety. I hadn't seen the shuttle launch depart, and she could have boarded it while my attention was focused on the first officer's report. If that were the case, I could only hope that she didn't run into Mutt and Jeff somewhere in Malacca Town.

Well, all right, Connell, I told myself wearily. Maria's gone and Kirby's gone and Mutt and Jeff are gone; the whole damned business is more or less finished with as far as you're concerned. Go to bed, get some sleep. Forget it.

I locked the cabin door, undressed, shut off the light, and got into the one bunk. My ribcage still ached, and I thought of going into the head and putting some ointment on the bruise. But I could feel sleep coming on, and torpor kept me from getting up and doing that.

If I had, I would have found out then, instead of the following morning, that everything I owned of minor value was missing.

# 4

I stood staring at the spot on the bathroom sink where I had put my leather carry-all case. It was a few minutes past 8 A.M., and I had been awakened by rain spattering against the cabin porthole and by the steady pitch and sway of the steamer. I had lain in the bunk for a time, gritty-eyed, body stiff and sore, and then I had gotten up and finally entered the head.

Understanding of what had happened to the case was immediate, and it was followed by a rush of bitter anger. I turned out of there and went to my closed suitcase on the second bunk and flipped the catches. Gone from it were some pieces of cheap men's jewelry in a chamois tie pouch, a brand-new wallet made out of hamadryad skin, and the new pair of jungle boots I had bought before leaving Singapore. In addition to my spare cache of some sixty Malay dollars, the carry-all had contained a gold-plated lighter which I rarely used any more, a copper-horseshoe good-luck charm, and a relatively expensive wristwatch which had a broken crystal and no longer ran. All of those missing articles were of course ones which could be sold or pawned quickly and easily.

I threw the suitcase shut, slapped it a couple of times in frustrated rage. The bitch, I thought; the damned avaricious little bitch! I had maybe saved her life, and offered her help and sanctuary, and she had repaid that by picking me clean. Like a vulture. Like a vampire sucking not blood but the milk of human kindness. Well, it was my own goddamn fault; I should have known better, I should have remembered that in Southeast Asia the predators are everywhere, guised in many forms, and things like gratitude and trust are nothing more than hollow words.

I had no doubts at all now that Maria had taken the Malacca shuttle launch last night—as much to escape from me as from Mutt and Jeff. But I put my clothes on and slammed out of there anyway, to seek confirmation. It took me fifteen minutes to get it; one of the crew members had noticed her standing with other main deck passengers during the time the launch was tied up at the float, and then he had seen her run down the gangway and board it just as it was preparing to pull out for the quay. He thought she'd looked a little frightened, he said.

Yeah.

For a while I stood on deck and watched the warm rain falling in a steady, sibilant hiss. A low-hanging mist partially obscured the line of jungle shoreward; what little light filtered through the ominously clouded sky was gray and cheerless. Most of my anger abated and was replaced by a melancholy depression as dark as the morning itself.

I went finally onto the bridge and into the pilothouse. As I'd expected, Holzmein had nothing further to report from Malacca; Mutt and Jeff had apparently gotten away clear. I considered reporting the theft of my belongings to Holzmein, and through him the Malacca police. But hell, what good would it do? Chances were Maria was no longer in Malacca, and even if she were, the authorities couldn't be counted on to expend much of an effort looking for her, not on what amounted to a charge of petty larceny. Unless, of course, I told them she was the one who had actually witnessed the deep-sixing of Kirby—but that would mean admitting I had lied to them originally. They wouldn't like that; it might even make them want to interview me personally. And I still had no desire for a session with the minions of local law.

So I left the pilothouse without saying anything about the theft, and went down to the dining room and ordered a cup of tea; I had no appetite for food. Over the tea and a sour-tasting cigarette, I remembered that I'd heard Maria tell the planter type she was bound for Kuala Lumpur. Maybe that was the truth and maybe it wasn't; but if it was, there was a possibility she could be located there. It seemed to me that petty theft was something you resorted to when you were broke, or close to it, and when you were a stranger to an area where you had no friends or contacts. She'd probably used most of her money for passage on the *Pangkor*, and she obviously hadn't gotten anything out of Phelps or Phillips. It was even possible that the reason he'd looked so disgruntled last night was that he'd caught her trying to steal from him too.

Another thing: the heavy makeup she wore, the overpronounced sway of her hips, and her come-on to the planter type were all indicative of either a tavern girl or a full-fledged whore. K.L. was a big place, but when you combined all these probable facts about her you could make a close guess as to her options, and narrow down the area of search considerably.

My best bet was to call a man I knew named Fordyce when I got into Kuala Lumpur. Fordyce was the one person

25

who could find a *sundal* of one kind or another looking for work in K.L. Given enough time, he could probably find anybody anywhere on the Malay Peninsula.

The things Maria had stolen were inconsequential in monetary terms, but no man likes to be suckered and victimized—and because of what I once was, I like it even less than most. That was one reason I wanted a confrontation with her. Another reason, perhaps the most important, was the copper-horseshoe good-luck charm and the relatively expensive watch that no longer ran. Both had been given to me by Pete Falco on the fifth anniversary of our partnership in Connell and Falco Transport, and I did not want to lose either one. They reminded me of a man and a friendship and a lot of good things that had not perished when Pete died three years ago on a lonely airstrip in a Penang Island jungle.

I first met Pete when we were both flying F-86 Sabre jets during the Korean War. Two years after it ended, when we were discharged from the service, we decided to stay on in the East—Pete because he was an orphan and liked the flavor of this part of the world, I because I had been Dear-Johned from my home in San Francisco and had nothing of any consequence waiting back in the States. He went to Burma and became a charter pilot, and I went to Kuala Lumpur and hooked in with a Belgian who ran a small air freight line. I was looking for a combination of excitement and money, and I found both with the Belgian. He supplied weapons to the Indonesians during their independence fight with the Dutch, and kept on supplying them during Sukarno's Confrontation with the Federation of Malaysia. For six years I made a total of seventy-nine blackout runs across the Strait of Malacca.

But the prospect of even more money—in the black-market smuggling of contraband and illicit art objects—decided me finally to move off on my own. Pete and I had kept in touch, and just about that time I'd gotten a letter from him saying that he had a chance to buy out a freight line on Singapore and wanting to know if I'd be interested in making it a partnership. It was made to order for what I had in mind, because Pete had a clean record and a reputation for honesty. In the beginning I kept the smuggling angle from him, handling that alone, but as I eventually began to make more connections than I could accommodate, I determined I would have to bring him in or allow a few of the more lucrative offers to pass by.

At first he wouldn't have any of it. But I kept after him, pushing and wheedling and tempting him with the money, and finally he consented to make a run with me. That run was to Penang, and we were carrying thirty thousand Straits dollars in contraband silk.

The man we were supposed to deliver the silk to, Spindello, assured me that the small airstrip was in good condition and would be well lighted for our past-midnight landing. It was neither. Despite Pete's vehement protests, I took the DC-3 down anyway. I could make it, I said. All I could think of was the money.

We crashed ten seconds after touchdown, when one of our wheels hit a hole in the badly pitted surface. The gas tank ruptured, and the high octane fuel ignited. The last thing I remembered was hearing Pete scream.

I awoke in a hospital in Wellesley Province three days later with a broken leg, a concussion and a few minor burns. I had been thrown clear, and found by a group of native workers attracted by the fire. Pete had never made it out of his seat.

Later, criminal charges were brought against me, but since the contraband silk had been burned beyond recognition, they didn't have enough evidence to convict me of anything. They did not even have enough to force me off of Singapore as an undesirable—not at that time, anyway. All they were able to do was to revoke my commercial license and place me on extended probation.

I think they expected me to move right back into the black market, or some other illegal enterprise, and were waiting for me to do that so they could tack my ass to the proverbial wall. But what they didn't know was that part of me had died along with Pete Falco; that all of a sudden money and adventure and the life-style the Italians call *la dolce vita* became meaningless; that guilt and a kind of belated but vivid self-perception had straightened out my head for the first time in my life and given me a whole new set of values. Everyone changes, but only a few are driven to a complete metamorphosis. Which is why most people refuse to believe it can happen, and why even now, after three years, former associates and government officials alike—with the exception of the Singapore cop named Tiong—warily consider me an irritating enigma.

But I know the truth, and that's all that matters. The past is dead and for the most part buried in a shallow grave in the back of my mind; there is only today and tomorrow. But as a kind of penitent reminder, three or four times a month the grave opens while I sleep and I relive in sharp detail that night on Penang—and wake sweating and trembling with the sound of Pete's screams in my ears. I think it's going to be that way for a long, long time to come . . .

I tasted my tea, and it might have been brewed from bilge water. I shoved the cup away and got up and exchanged the dining room for the ship's saloon. It was only 9 A.M., much too early to think about getting drunk. Still, with the depression sitting heavily on my mind, I sat at the bar anyway and went to work on the *Pangkor's* supply of Anchor beer.

# 5

At noon, in the warm driving rain and pitching seas, we came through the mangrove islands lying off the coast and into the harbor of Port Swettenham. Anchored fishing boats rolled and bobbed and twisted outside a network of spindly gray piers, like natives performing a silent, ritualistic dance; and through the downpour the steep tile roofs and terra-cottaed walls of the town had a desolate appearance. Above the green hills to the north, rays of sunlight slanted down through rifts in the cloud cover and there was the suggestion of a rainbow.

I'd had seven or eight beers in the saloon, but lack of food and the constant roll of the steamer had made my stomach dangerously queasy long before I'd gotten any kind of edge on. Finally I had returned to my cabin and lain down for a time, until I felt better. Only then my head had begun a steady throbbing. Welcome back to the Malay Peninsula, Connell, I thought. Rain and a sorry gut and a headache and assorted bruises and half your belongings gone: some homecoming, all right. Some day.

When the launch came I was standing on deck with my suitcase. I hurried down the gangway and found a seat inside where it was dry. Dirty-silver spume combined with the rain to make the shuttle's windows opaque as we jounced in to the main quay. Once we had tied up I asked one of the crew where the bus station was, got simple directions, and set off walking through the black deluge. I was soaked when I reached the station. After I had gotten my ticket for K.L.—the next bus was at two—I went through a door marked *Laki* and changed clothes.

My stomach began to feel queasy again, and I thought I'd better get something to eat. I put my suitcase into a locker, found a restaurant, and ate shashlik and rice and didn't drink anything. The rain had stopped when I came out, and the clouds were scudding south, and you could see the hazy white glare of the sun overhead. It was beginning to get hot; steam rose from the wet streets in thin smoky wisps. I wandered around Port Swettenham's small business district in preference to sitting in the station waiting room, and gradually some of the depression began to lift. I was feeling almost agreeable again when I returned to the station at five minutes before two and boarded the crowded bus for Kuala Lumpur.

I found a cramped seat in the rear. The bus wasn't air-conditioned, and you couldn't open the windows, and the smell of human bodies was thick and faintly sour. I unbuttoned my bush jacket down the front and sat there marinating in my own sweat, thoughts fallow, as we got underway.

The land between Port Swettenham and K.L. is flattish for the most part, with lush green vegetation and cultivated rubber stretching all the way to emerald mountains north and south, broken only by occasional brown farmland. I dozed as we passed through it, lulled by the heat, but woke when we came into Kuala Lumpur at three-thirty.

I hadn't been in K.L. since 1967, but I knew the population had topped three hundred thousand, and I noticed without pleasure that there were more modern skyscraper hotels and office buildings, more new suburbs and housing developments—all at the expense of what had been virgin jungle only a few years ago. But the overall look and feel of the city hadn't changed. It was, like Singapore, still a heterogenous blending of races: Chinese, Caucasians, Eurasians, Malay men wearing *baju* coats and velvet *songkoks* on their heads, saffron-robed Sinhalese monks, turbaned and bearded Sikhs, barefoot Tamils, gaily dressed Kadayans. And the venerable Moorish-style buildings and Chinese temples and domed and minareted Malay mosques still gave the main sections a kind of enticing Old World atmosphere.

When I left the bus at the main depot, I hunted up a trishaw and told the runner to take me to the Prinsep Hotel on Jalan Tioman. It was an antiquated, four-story building not far from Old Chinatown, which had undergone a facelift of sorts since I'd last seen it and which catered more to a lower middle class native population than to the tourist trade. Since in his letter Quayles had indicated a willingness to send a car to K.L. for me, I had wired for a reservation and then written Quayles that that was where I would be.

The trishaws have no fixed prices, except for the tourists, and I spent a couple of minutes traditionally haggling with my driver over the fare. Inside the Prinsep's small lobby, I gave my name to a tall Malay desk clerk. He found my reservation and put me in a room on the third floor: tiny, cramped, with a too-short bed and bilious green louvered shutters; bathroom facilities, such as they were, down the hall and to your left.

I went out again almost immediately, walked downstairs, and looked around the lobby for a public telephone. Not

31

surprisingly, there wasn't any. So I left the hotel and wandered up Jalan Tioman until I came to a bar that had both a phone and a local directory.

The last time I had seen Fordyce was more than four years before, when he'd come down to Singapore on some business or other. At that time he'd still owned six or seven nightclubs of questionable repute in K.L., including a place called The Lair that doubled as his office. A lot can happen in four years—nobody knew that better than I—but, Fordyce being Fordyce, I would have given any odds that nothing had altered his path of existence. He was a shrewd, likable, less than scrupulous Welshman, reared in London and twenty-five years transplanted in Malaysia, who had a finger in several of K.L.'s quasi-legitimate pies; who could if he felt like it charm the knickers off a bluenosed English Lady; who gave lavish parties at his villa near the Lake Gardens and contributed time and money to local charities and benefits; who sported an incredible handlebar mustache and had a passion for Aston-Martins and Eurasian wives, at last count having collected three of the former and, bigamously, two of the latter. I'd met him while I was living high in K.L. and we'd become relatively good friends. We would no longer have much in common, of course, but I knew he wouldn't hesitate to do me the favor I was going to ask of him.

I looked up the number of The Lair, dialed it—and Fordyce's familiar, rumbling voice answered on the fifth ring. I said, "Hello, you bloody heathen. This is Dan Connell."

There was a pause, and then he made an explosive chortling sound. "Dan! By the Queen's arse, it's been a long time. Last I heard of you, you were in a bit of a bind over a crackup on Penang. I was beginning to think your ruddy bum was rotting away in a quod somewhere. Where're you calling from, Yank? Not here in K.L.?"

"K.L. it is."

"By the Queen's arse. Business or pleasure trip?"

"Business," I told him, but I didn't elaborate.

"How long will you be staying?"

"Just until early tomorrow."

"Pity. Well, you'll come for *satay* tonight. We're having a small party afterward, and there'll be some fine quiff on hand."

"Sounds good," I said, "but I don't think I can make it, Forry." I would have liked to see him, and I would have liked a woman, but if I accepted the invitation, there would be a lot of questions I didn't care to answer and a lot of reminiscing about a past I just wanted to keep buried. Too, I had been to a number of Fordyce's "small parties," and they were the kind where anything goes; one I had attended had lasted four days. The prospect of an evening of drinking and wenching in the old style left me cold. "I've got some things to do tonight. But I'll be back in K.L. again before long. We'll get together then."

"I should bloody well hope so. Dan'l lad, what've you been up to these past four years? Still flying about in those ruddy metal birds?"

"Not anymore," I said shortly. "Listen, Forry, can you do me a favor?"

"Name it, Yank."

I explained briefly about the theft, omitting specific details and telling him only that Maria Velasquez had stolen some "valuable personal items"; then I gave him a careful description of her, and my guess that she was probably a tavern girl looking for work here in Kuala Lumpur.

Fordyce found the situation humorous. He had always been fond of affecting an exaggerated Cockney accent, and he did it now, saying, "Blimey, an old 'and like yerself gettin' robbed by a bleedin' 'ore—it ain't t' be believed. Yer slippin', ducky; yer gettin' old. Well, Forry'll see wot 'e can do. Where're you styin'? The Merlin?"

The Merlin was one of K.L.'s best hotels. I said, "No, I'm

33

. . . with a friend. But I'm leaving now and I won't be back until late. Can I give you a call at home later tonight?"

"Yer can." He gave me his home number. "We're still at the syme place; if yer can fynd the time, drop round, hear? Me old lydies'd luv to see yer again too."

"Sure," I said. "Thanks, Forry."

"Right-o. Give yer friend a stroke fer old Forry, wot?" Chuckling, he rang off.

When I came out of the bar, I found that I was hungry again and wandered over through The Embankment and Market Square to the Central Market. It was jammed with tourists and hawkers, buying and selling everything from medicinal Chinese herbs to exotic Malaysian potables; from live iguanas in cages to mounted displays of brilliantly colored butterflies; from Kelantan silverware to Balinese black *bidri* wood carvings. I bought myself pork curry and small, spiny rambutan fruits, then drifted over to the juncture of the Klang and Gombak rivers, where the original city was founded more than a hundred years ago.

Once darkness settled, I returned to the Prinsep by way of the *padang* in the center of K.L., thinking that I would have a shower and rest for an hour or so before calling Fordyce again. The lobby was deserted when I entered at seven-thirty, and the Malay desk clerk was sound asleep in a rattan safari chair. I climbed the stairs to the third floor and went along the dimly lit corridor to my room.

The door was standing six inches ajar.

Lips pulling in against my teeth, I leaned forward and peered through the slit. Darkness shrouded the room, although a pale shaft of early moonlight coming in through one of the open-shuttered windows gave substance to the shadows of furniture. I put my hand flat against the surface of the door and shoved it inward. There was a sharp sound as it met the wall inside; then, only silence.

After a moment I went in cautiously and put on the lights.

34

The room was empty, but it was goddamn evident someone had been there. The mattress had been pulled off the bed, and the only chair was overturned, and all the drawers had been pulled out of the dresser and nightstand. My suitcase was on the floor, open like a yawning mouth. Everything that had been in it lay scattered from wall to wall.

I said "Shit!" savagely, and slammed the door. Then I picked up the suitcase and threw it on the bedsprings and went through the wreckage to find out what was missing this time.

The answer was nothing—not a single damned thing.

# 6

I didn't know what to think.

I righted the chair and sat on it, staring over at the bed. Sneak thieves are a problem in any large city in Southeast Asia, particularly this close to a Chinese settlement; but a sneak thief would sure as hell have made off with the suitcase instead of taking the time to go through it here—and one would hardly have bothered to ransack the room itself. I'd been hit now twice in the space of twenty-four hours, and that was stretching coincidence a little too far; besides, the way my things had been gone through seemed to indicate a search for something. But what? And who? And why?

There were no apparent answers to any of those questions, and because there weren't, the sharp anger inside me was impotent. God *damn* it! I stood up, kicked the chair to one side, and had a look at the door latch. Faint scratches on the brass: whoever it was had picked the lock. Some lock; a six-year-old kid could have picked it with a hairpin. I

36

stepped out into the hall, banged the door shut again, and went downstairs. The Malay clerk was still sleeping behind the desk. I got hold of his shoulders and shook him awake.

"Listen," I said, "somebody broke into my room and ransacked it while I was out."

He stared at me with wide, dark eyes.

"Did anybody come in asking for me?"

"No, *tuan*. No one asked for you."

"No calls either?"

He shook his head.

"How long have you been sleeping here?"

"I do not know, *tuan*. Not long . . ."

"Yeah," I said.

"Was anything stolen? Should I call the *polis*?"

"Forget it. Just get someone up there to straighten up the room and check the lock on the door."

"Yes, *tuan*. Right away, *tuan*."

I turned away from him and got out of there and went to the bar where I had called Fordyce earlier. I drank a couple of Anchor beers, calming down; then I crossed to the public telephone and dialed the number Fordyce had given me for his villa.

A Chinese woman answered, asked my name, and then told me to wait. I could hear vague sounds of laughter and music: the party was already in full swing. When Fordyce came on the wire I said, "Dan Connell, Forry. Anything on Maria Velasquez?"

"By the Queen's arse, Yank," he said, "this is your lucky day. Toy called me an hour ago: seems your bird came round to the Mandarin suckin' up to him for a spot. He put her on the dangle, and she gave him her address to get in touch with her—in bloody whoretown on the north bank of the Klang. Like as not you'll find her there now, waiting for word."

The Mandarin was a tavern which catered to laborers off

the river lighters and to fringe-of-the-law types and occasional slumming tourists. Toy, I supposed, was its owner or manager, although the name was not one I remembered.

I said, "What's the address, Forry?"

He gave it to me. Then, tongue in cheek, "Go gentle on the muff, Yank. Toy says she's a flippin' peach."

"A lot Toy knows."

Chuckling sounds. "Cor, 'e's a bleedin' lemon ternight, 'e is!" Fordyce said in that damned Cockney accent. "What 'e needs is a birdie wot'll ruffle 'is feather fer 'im. Come round to the party after yer've seen Maria, and old Forry'll fix yer up right fine."

"The hell I will," I said. "Penicillin shots cost too goddamn much in K.L."

He roared. "Serious now, Dan'l. Come round if you can."

"Sure," I said. "But if not, I'll keep in touch. Thanks again, Forry."

I caught a taxi outside. The Tamil driver made liberal use of his horn as he took us through the warm, scented night to the Klang River, across it and into what Fordyce had called "whoretown." It wasn't exactly that. What it was was a kind of lower class native area, not rundown enough to be termed a slum or ghetto; a lot of tavern girls and prostitutes had always lived there because of cheap accommodations, which was the reason for the "whoretown" appellation.

The place Maria Velasquez had rented was little more than an atap-roofed shack, one of a long row of similar dwellings squatting close together with their backsides on the muddy bank of the river. Chamadora palms and casuarina trees grew sparsely in the area; wild shrubs and vines and weeds were more prevalent. Light shone behind rattan blinds in the single front window.

I paid the Tamil driver and went along a short path paralleling a high *dadap* hedge that separated this property from the neighbor on the left. Somebody in one of the nearby shacks had a parrot, and the thing was screeching obscenities in Malay and then imitating a laugh as if it thought itself very funny. You could smell the river odors of garbage and fish.

When I rapped on the front door, footsteps sounded immediately from within, light and quick. She was smiling when she opened up, because she was expecting Toy or someone else from the Mandarin.

I said, "Hello, Maria."

The smile froze into a rictus on her too-red lips, and one hand came up involuntarily to her throat in an almost theatrical gesture of recognition and sudden fright. She took a step backward and tried to pull the door closed. I jerked it out of her hand and swung it open wider and went in there, causing her to back-pedal rapidly. She was wearing a short, brilliant-orange cheongsam, and the slit in one side reached almost to her hip. She had got the dress at least two sizes too small and it bunched under her breasts and made them look like enormous *semangka* melons. The whole effect was designed to impress the hell out of Toy, but I wasn't Toy and I wasn't impressed.

"Let's talk, Maria," I said. "About the things you pinched from my cabin on board the *Pangkor*."

She was uncertain about which way to play it; I was pretty much an unknown quantity to her. I watched her grapple with the problem for a moment, trying to read what was on my face. Finally she decided lying wouldn't buy her anything but that a show of contriteness might. She sat down on a frayed settee and clasped her hands like a naughty child.

"How are you to find me?" she asked the floor.

"Never mind that."

"You must believe, I am not really thief. I am needing money and I am afraid of those two men and I do not want to stay on the boat." Her eyes came up plaintively. "You understand, *Ginoong?* I do what I did in a bad moment."

39

"Sure," I said. "A bad moment."

"I hate myself for it because you help me, and I am truly sorry. But life is so difficult . . ."

I didn't say anything. She may have been at least partially sincere—life out here was difficult, all right—but I was in no mood to give her the benefit of the doubt. As the old maxim has it: once bitten, twice shy.

Maria sighed and lowered her gaze again. "Those men, they are captured?"

"No. They got away in Malacca harbor."

"But I make sure they are not on the little boat . . ."

"They swam ashore. You're damned lucky you didn't run into them."

She shivered faintly. "I am truly sorry," she said again.

"Where are the things you took?"

Hesitation.

"Come on, Maria," I said. "Come *on*."

"I . . . they are here."

"All of them?"

"Almost all."

"You've already sold some things, is that it?"

"Yes," in a small voice.

"What?"

"The cigarette lighter, and the boots."

"Where? Here in K.L.?"

"No. To a man I meet in Malacca. On the street."

"And the sixty Malay dollars?"

"I . . . I use it to come here by train."

"Not the whole sixty you didn't."

"I must pay a part to rent this living place . . ."

"Yeah. Okay, get the rest of the stuff."

She nodded eagerly. "Yes, *Ginoong*," she said, and stood and went across to a bedroom archway. I walked over there too, to make sure she didn't try to go out a window, and watched her rummage through her open bag on a quilt-covered daybed. She came up with my carry-all and the chamois tie pouch, and brought them out to me. I opened the case and sifted through it. The copper-horseshoe good-luck charm and the watch were there; so were all the other things. The sack contained, as it had before, my few inexpensive pieces of men's jewelry.

"What will you do now?" Maria asked softly.

I just looked at her.

"You will not take me to the police, yes?" She put one hand up to the side of her breast, cupping it in what was supposed to be a provocative invitation. "I will do much for you if you do not take me to the police. I will—"

"You won't do any damned thing at all," I said harshly. "I'm not going to take you to the police, even though that's just what I ought to do, and I'm not going to touch you any way at all. But remember this, Maria: if you're smart, you'll keep your hands off other people's belongings; the next guy might be a hell of a lot less charitable than I am."

I turned away so that I wouldn't have to look at her relief, walked over to the door, and slammed out. I'd been pretty easy on her, all right, but the gold cigarette lighter and jungle boots and the sixty Malay dollars were minor losses; I had gotten back the items that really mattered to me—the good-luck charm and the wristwatch. I'm not the kind of man who slaps women around, and turning Maria in to the authorities was out for the old and good reason of nonin-volvement. Besides, large or small revenge doesn't solve or salve a thing. The bed Maria Velasquez had made for herself was, in a way, punishment enough for her.

Thinking this, I reached the street and started along it to the west. A leafy kapok tree cast thick shadows over the walkway, and when I passed under it a man stepped out suddenly and blocked my way, startling me, causing me to pull up short. He just stood there, looking at me from two feet away. It was dark, but not so dark that I couldn't see his face clearly.

Mutt—the short, mustached one from the *Pangkor*.

# 7

I said "What the hell?" and took a step toward him. There was a sound behind me in that instant, and too late I remembered Jeff; a hand looped around my chest, jerking me backward and to one side, up against the trunk of the kapok tree. I fought his grip, dropping the sack and the carry-all. Mutt came up and caught my free left arm and pinned it against my body. He had a knife in his other hand, and he put the point of it against my lower jaw. I stopped struggling.

"We'll have a talk now," he said.

"Talk about what?"

"The Red Fire, of course."

"The what?"

"Perhaps you don't know it by that name, but you know what I mean. If you wish to stay alive, you will cooperate with us."

"Listen, you bastard—"

Abruptly he moved the knife down under my chin,

drawing it sideways. The point edge was razor sharp and it sliced into the soft flesh there. I felt a quick stinging pain—and that was the final injustice in a day of injustices; a man can only take so much. All my pent-up anger came boiling to the surface, and I stopped thinking restraint and caution. I stopped thinking at all, letting my reflexes and a twenty-year, military-taught knowledge of karate take over.

I twisted both my head and my body down and to my left, pulling Jeff with me as I came below the level of the knife. At the same time I brought my right knee up toward the apex of Mutt's legs in a short pistonlike movement. It took him on the fleshy part of the upper thigh, pitching him off-balance. His grip on my left arm had been loose to begin with and I broke it easily an instant before my knee connected, using an upward snapping motion. I unlocked the elbow and drove it back into Jeff's ribs, heard him grunt, felt his hold across my chest relax; locked it again and bunched and slightly cupped my fingers, with the thumb curled out almost at a right angle. I could use my right arm then, as well, and I jabbed Jeff in the lower belly with that elbow, breaking free of him; simultaneously, I lunged forward with my left arm, and the stiffened fingers caught Mutt in the soft area beneath the chin.

But that last blow was glancing: it knocked him down but it didn't disable him, and it didn't make him release the knife. I spun to one side on the balls of my feet. Jeff was bent over, looking up at me with his lips flattened wolfishly against his teeth, digging in the pocket of his jacket. Mutt had gotten to one knee and was trying to stand.

They were five or six paces apart, and the way it looked they had two knives instead of one. I'd been lucky so far, but I knew I would be a damned fool to press it. The intelligent thing to do was to get the hell away from them; I put a tight check on my anger and did just that.

Pivoting, I ran back toward Maria's shack—the only

direction open to me. I cut between it and the neighboring building on this side. I could hear that parrot screeching and laughing nearby, now in an alarmed way, but no one else seemed to have taken notice of what was happening. Damp earth gave way to thick greenish mud as I came out on the river bank, and I slowed to keep from slipping down. Scudding clouds had momentarily eclipsed the moon, but visibility was still good. I saw that the bank stretched out in a long jagged line in both directions, dotted with dugout canoes and the remains of an oxcart and bamboo fishnet stakes; there were no trees, no vegetation of any density, nothing to offer a shielded path of escape.

Mutt and Jeff had escaped by swimming last night, and now, bitterly, it was my turn. Because I had only one real choice: the black, refuse-littered waters of the Klang.

Fifty yards to the east, a rickety pier built on pilings extended a short distance into the river like a dark finger pointing at the opposite shore. Two small deserted-looking, shallow-draft junks and a native fishing outrigger rode at anchor beyond it. I ran that way, reached the pier, jumped up on it. Gnats and mosquitoes swarmed around my head; I heard a fish leap and splash off on my left, the monotonous murmuring of the river current. When I looked back over my shoulder Mutt and Jeff were less than forty yards away, running side by side through the mud.

The pier boarding was old and splintered in places, and it groaned and creaked as I ran along it. Without slowing, I went off the end in a low flat dive. The water was cool, heavily silted, and I could taste a sweetish, oily pollution as it folded over me. I fought to keep from gagging, kicked down and at an angle toward the nearest of the two unlighted junks. Pressure mounted rapidly in my lungs. I stayed down as long as I could, swimming blind, then twisted my body and let myself buoy up slowly to break the surface. Taking air in silent inhalations, I looked back toward the pier.

45

The two of them had come up on it and were stopped halfway out. With the moon still hidden, I didn't think they'd managed to locate me yet. I took myself under again, not diving so as to prevent a carrying sound and telltale ripples. My shoes were waterlogged and as heavy as metal weights, but I didn't want to take the time to get them off and I didn't want to lose them. I kept my muscles relaxed, letting the current carry me forward as much as the movement of my arms and legs.

When I surfaced for air a second time, I was thirty yards from the junk and behind a drifting, storm-severed palm frond. Mutt and Jeff were down off the pier now, the short one gesticulating. They still hadn't seen me. The palm frond nudged my chin, and I slid under once more and swam just below the surface. This time the junk was between me and the shore when I came up. I used a silent breast stroke to the high arrowhead prow, then around it to where I could see part of the bank and to where a rusted anchor chain hung down into the river. I caught hold of the chain, treading water lightly, watching Mutt prowl abreast of the junk and then stop and stare outward with his head pushed forward like a marsh bird's. I didn't see Jeff at all.

Time passed, and Mutt kept on moving back and forth and staring out into the river. My legs began to ache; the Klang seemed to have gotten colder, and the stench of it was overpowering. Come on, you bastard, I thought, give it up. As far as you're concerned I'm long gone.

Finally I saw him walk back toward the pier, stop for another look, and then increase his pace away from the river and up the bank. I released the chain and eased forward for a better viewing angle. He was alone; there was still no sign of Jeff. A moment later he disappeared along the side of Maria's shack.

Maria, I thought.

Oh Jesus, I had forgotten all about her—and the two of

them had seen me enter the dwelling and seen me come out again. They could have added that up to mean I'd given whoever lived there this Red Fire they were after, or that that person knew where it was. Mutt could have sent Jeff to brace her; that would explain why I hadn't seen the tall one in the past few minutes. And if he had, and if they recognized Maria as the witness to their deep-sixing of Kirby from on board the *Pangkor*. . . .

Urgency formed inside me, knotted the muscles in my stomach. I had no damned desire to play hero by going up against the two of them again—I still wanted noninvolvement more than anything else—but I knew I couldn't run out on somebody whose life was in jeopardy, even if it meant putting my own life right back on the line. I had enough on my conscience; it wouldn't stand any more.

I kicked away from the junk and swam in a strong, silent crawl cross-current toward the pier. The moon was still partially obscured by the moving clouds. Using the pilings to shield my body, I stood up in shallow water near the outer end and then waded in quickly. When I cleared the river I ran humped over up the bank to the rear wall of the nearest darkened shack, put my back against it, and began visually searching the ground there for something I could use as a weapon.

A few feet away a slender black shape lay in the mud, and when I stepped over and bent to it, I saw that it was a piece of gnarled driftwood shaped like a Scottish walking stick. I caught it up. It was a little unwieldy, but it had plenty of weight; it would do. Turning, I moved in against the building wall again. Front or rear approach? Front, I thought. There's more cover out there.

I went along the side of the shack. A woman made a high-pitched moaning cry in the adjacent dwelling, the kind of cry some people make at intense sexual orgasm; there were no other sounds except for those made by insects and the

47

murmuring river. Keeping to pockets of heavy darkness, I ran across a weed-choked front yard and then several contiguous yards. When I neared the bordering *dadap* hedge I'd noticed earlier, I moved diagonally toward where it ended at the sidewalk.

I crouched down there and peered around—and an automobile engine coughed to life somewhere nearby. Head-lamps came on then, across the street and maybe fifty yards down the block. The car was small and low-slung, I could see that much, but without benefit of moonlight I couldn't make out the model or color or number of occupants. Gears meshed and it pulled away from the curb burning rubber. Gathering speed, it vanished almost instantly from my line of vision.

My hand tightened around the length of driftwood, and I moved out around the hedge to where I could see Maria's shack. Light still shone behind the rattan blinds—and light shone, too, in a bright wedge at the door. It was standing partially open.

A chill shimmered along the saddle of my back, clung there with the soaked material of my bush jacket. That goddamn parrot had started up again, cursing and laughing and squawking, but from the shack itself there was only silence. The yard shadows, and those along the street and beneath the kapok tree farther down, were solid.

I straightened up and ran along the hedge until I came parallel with the front wall. Then I cut across under the window and caught the door jamb with my free hand and swung inside through the opening, the driftwood club held out from chest level. But when I'd had my first clear look at the interior, I lowered the wood and let it hang heavily at my side. The chill on my back deepened and contracted my shoulder muscles in a small convulsive shudder.

I was too late, all right. Minutes too late.

Maria Velasquez lay sprawled at the settee near the

window, hips on the floor, torso twisted and head flung back at a grotesque angle against the cushions. Her eyes bulged and she'd bitten through her lower lip; a thin trickle of blood, like an exposed and ugly red vein, traced down over her chin and along the column of her throat and into the high collar of her bright orange cheongsam.

One of those two sons of bitches had snapped her neck as easily and cruelly as though it had been the stem of an exotic flower.

Anger made my mouth dry and brassy as I looked down at her. She'd been a tramp and a petty thief, but she'd also been young and pretty and spirited, and maybe someday she would have met somebody decent and learned decency herself; maybe she, too, would have undergone one of those rare and complete metamorphoses. Instead she was a broken lump of clay, with no more somedays or somebodies—brutally dead for a minor sin of her own and a major sin of others.

I raised my eyes and looked at the shabby, sparsely furnished room. They'd searched it quickly and destructively: chairs overturned, drawers pulled out of an old standing wall cabinet, Maria's pitifully few personal belongings scattered across the floor; in the bedroom, the daybed mattress slashed and bleeding white stuffing. They hadn't had time to question her extensively, either verbally or with their hands and their goddamn knives. So it could be she'd convinced them immediately that she had no knowledge of the Red Fire they were looking for, or it could be they'd killed her in frustration or the heat of the moment, or it could be they'd killed her without bothering to ask questions at all. It didn't really matter now; it just didn't matter.

I went out through the door without touching it, pushed it closed with my foot, and tossed the driftwood club into the *dadap* hedge. Then I cut through the weeds to the left, until I came into the shadows cast by the kapok tree. Under a pale street lamp on the far corner, two young Chinese whores were holding an animated business conference with a white-uniformed seaman; the street was otherwise deserted. I moved in against the kapok's trunk and dropped to one knee on the damp, grassy ground.

My carry-all case was lying upside down in a patch of thistle, zippered open and empty. Mutt and Jeff hadn't forgot the things I'd dropped, either; it had probably been Jeff who had gone through them, even before confronting Maria. I ran my hands through the wet grass and located and pocketed the chamois pouch, also empty, and then the wristwatch, and finally the good-luck charm—all flung down in anger when examination had yielded negative results. At first I couldn't find the letter from Martin Quayles, and I wanted that because it had my name on it and the police would undoubtedly canvass the yard. There wasn't anything else that could put them on to me among the contents of the carry-all and the pouch. That letter could also put Mutt and Jeff on to my ultimate destination in Malaya, I thought, and I was beginning to have qualms that they'd read it and carried it off when I saw the wad of crumpled paper on the far side of the trunk. I caught it up and smoothed it out enough to see that it was the letter. I released a soft breath and put it into my pocket with the other things. I straightened up then, the carry-all under my arm, and went away rapidly along the empty sidewalk.

I hadn't had time for speculation until now, and I gave my mind over to it as I walked. Who and what were Mutt and Jeff? I had no idea, except for the fact that they were, along with whatever else, cold-blooded murderers. What was this Red Fire they seemed to think I had? Again, no idea; the appellation didn't mean a thing to me. Why did they think I had it, or knew where it was? Kirby—yeah, there was no doubt it had something to do with Kirby. Well, were they after me because Kirby had told them I had the Red Fire? That didn't add up. Why would he have wilfully told them a lie that signed his own death warrant? And yet, why else would they have dumped him into the Strait last night?

Plenty of questions, but damned few answers. Christ!

All right, how had Mutt and Jeff found me here in K.L.? That, at least, wasn't so difficult to figure. After they'd swum ashore in Malacca, all they had had to do was to rent or steal a car and drive overland to Port Swettenham—if it had been necessary, to each of the *Pangkor's* scheduled stops—and then watch unobtrusively until I finally disembarked. It would have been no problem for them, since you can travel much faster by land than by sea. And it would have been no problem for them, either, to follow me to Kuala Lumpur and the Prinsep Hotel. They were the ones who had searched my room tonight, of course; a fast look at the register without disturbing the Malay's sleep would have given them my room number. And when they hadn't found what they were looking for, they'd waited and trailed me out here and jumped me the first chance they had.

It seemed likely enough that from Maria's shack they had gone straight back to the Prinsep, to set up a vigil; they wouldn't have any other way of locating me. Which bloody well meant I didn't intend to return there tonight or at all. I had enough money in my wallet to take another room somewhere. To be on the safe side I would have to call Martin Quayles, I thought, and cancel the car. Then, in the morning, I could get in touch with the Prinsep and make an arrangement for getting my suitcase, and find my own way to the Union Jack.

Six blocks from Maria's shack I came into a small business district. There was a public street telephone on one corner, and I entered that and dialed the number of the police. When I was sure the man who answered spoke English, I said, "Listen closely. A woman named Maria Velasquez has been murdered on Limau Road, number eighty. She was killed by two men; I don't know their names, but I can tell you what they look like."

The cop's voice chattered at me, asking identification.

"Never mind that. Just listen." I gave him detailed descriptions of Mutt and Jeff. "There's the possibility you'll find them somewhere on the six-hundred block of Jalan Tioman; I'd check the area carefully if I were you."

I hung up in the middle of another demand for my name.

The information operator located a number for Martin Quayles—it was listed at Kuala Ba, a village not far from his estate—but when I had another operator ring it for me, we couldn't get a connection. That happens all too often in Malaysia, particularly in outlying areas; the telephone system is something a hell of a lot less than sophisticated. It might be hours before I could get through, and I couldn't risk standing around in a telephone booth looking the way I did. I would have to try again later.

Across the street was a small, neon-lit *kedai minum*. I went over there and through a crowd of noisy patrons into the men's room. I had some mixed feelings about taking myself out of the whole vicious business—desire for noninvolvement struggling with rage at what I'd been put through and the brutal death of Maria Velasquez—but I knew it was the only intelligent choice. I'd have been gambling my freedom by going to the police directly, and gambling my life by playing a fool's game of personal reprisal. If there was justice in the world, and I believed that most of the time, in one way or another, there was, then Mutt and Jeff would get theirs. Sooner or later, they would get theirs.

I used paper towels to clean off the thicker patches of mud from my jacket and trousers; the garments themselves had dried out somewhat in the warmth of the night. Then I cleaned off my shoes, washed my face and hands, and combed my hair. I still looked and smelled like a derelict, but there were hotels in Old Chinatown where I would not have any trouble getting a room. Tomorrow I could buy some cheap new clothing.

After leaving the bar, I found a trishaw halfway down the next block. The runner looked at me suspiciously, but when I produced a handful of Malay dollars and told him I'd accidentally fallen into the river, he shrugged in a way that said he knew all about drunken American tourists and allowed me to climb up.

My watch read midnight—it still ran, even though it was a cheap Japanese import—when he reached Jalan Minyak, in the heart of Old Chinatown. I got off there and went down a narrow side street and entered the first hotel I saw, a seedy-looking place sandwiched between an herb shop and a noodle factory. The Chinese clerk looked at me stoically until I put money down in front of him, and then he didn't look at me at all.

For one Malay dollar he let me use his telephone, and I tried again to get through to Quayles. There was still no connection. This time my bilingual operator said she thought there was minor trouble with the lines in the Kuala Ba area, owing to the recent storm. She had no idea when things would return to normal.

So now what? Try him again in the morning. And if I still couldn't get through? Well, maybe I could chance using the driver after all. I could tell the Prinsep to have him pick up my suitcase and rendezvous with me somewhere else in K.L.

There wasn't really much risk involved, and I didn't want to start off bad with Quayles by failing to meet his driver if the driver did make the trip in.

The room the Chinese gave me was on the second floor rear, and it was little more than a cell: a single bed, a dresser with a whore's type of washbasin on top, a rickety chair, and a black, immense-antennaed longicorn beetle on one wall. Chinese voices and the click of mah-jongg tiles came from a neighboring room, and from somewhere far off the crashing of cymbals and gongs. I locked the door, threw the key and my carry-all onto the dresser, and emptied my pockets of change, comb, matches and soggy cigarettes. I got undressed and laid my clothing over the window sill, leaving the shutters open, and then laid myself down on the bed.

It took me a long time to find sleep, because I kept seeing Maria Velasquez's body and that ugly trail of blood running down from her mouth into the collar of the orange cheongsam. And when I slept at last, I dreamed again of the flaming crash of the DC-3 on Penang, and heard Pete Falco screaming . . . and screaming . . . and screaming . . .

# 9

The man who answered the phone at the Prinsep the following morning had a high, reedy voice, so I knew it wasn't the Malay who had been on duty the previous day. I told him my name, and he recognized it immediately. He was the day manager, he said, and he had been informed of the outrageous attack on my room and wished to offer his sincerest apologies. Hotels like the Prinsep didn't want police trouble either. I cut him off halfway through his regrets to ask if there had been anyone around inquiring about me, if there were any messages. The answers to both questions were negative.

Minutes earlier I'd tried to call Quayles again, but the phone lines in the Kuala Ba area were apparently still down. I had decided, then, to meet the Union Jack's driver as planned, though of course not at the Prinsep. I told the reedy voice about the driver and issued instructions for the handing over of my luggage. The driver was to meet me at the Masjid Negara or National Mosque, in front of the grand hall; I described what I was wearing. And under no circumstances was that information to be given to anyone else. The reedy voice assured me everything would be taken care of exactly as I wished.

After ringing off I turned away from the wall phone, which was in a bar two blocks from the hotel where I'd spent the night, and went back to my table for another cup of breakfast tea. I had gotten up at eight, to the cries of street hawkers; my clothes had dried completely and I had dressed and gone out and found an inexpensive clothing store. I bought and changed into a cheap bush jacket and a pair of heavy denims, and had the owner wrap my other things, as well as the carry-all, into a bundle. Then I hunted up a copy of the K.L. edition of the *Straits-Times*—I almost never read the newspapers anymore, but the jade figurine incident in Singapore had taught me a hard lesson that there were times when you couldn't afford not to read them—and took it with me into a barber shop. I had scanned the paper while a fat Chinese scraped beard stubble from my face with a dull razor, but there was nothing in it about the murder of Maria Velasquez. I would have to check later editions once I was settled in at the Union Jack.

When I finished my second cup of tea I got a package of cigarettes from the barman, and then I stepped out again into the bright morning heat. I made my way slowly through the noisy Chinatown crowds, beneath jutting balconies and a multicolored array of laundry draped like limp flags from long bamboo poles. My mood was not good; the events of the past two days, and Maria's death in particular, had re-created the kind of depression I'd felt on the *Pangkor* the previous morning, and destroyed most of my anticipation of the overseer's position on Quayles's rubber estate.

It was after eleven when I got to the National Mosque, an elegant, ultramodern Muslim house of prayer and meditation swarming with irreverent tourists. I might have picked a

57

less crowded place to meet the Union Jack's driver, but I'd wanted a location that was both well known and in close proximity to the Prinsep. We'd find one another, I thought, without any trouble.

And we did—or rather, she found me.

The fact that it was a she was something of a surprise. I was standing at the foot of the grand hall steps, smoking and watching the cars pass, and I saw the dark green open jeep pull over a few yards away and the girl alone behind the wheel; but since I was reasonably expecting a man, I gave both only a cursory glance. A moment later the girl got out, stood surveying the area, and then took off a pair of tinted sunglasses and approached me and said, "Mr. Daniel Connell?" in a voice tinged with irritation.

I turned to face her fully. "Yes?"

Gray-green eyes studied me critically, and were not in the least impressed. She was in her mid-twenties, slender and deeply tanned with close-cropped blonde hair and a stiff-backed carriage; dressed in a green short-sleeved bush-style jacket and slacks tucked into high jungle boots; wearing a dark coral bracelet on one wrist but no rings of any kind. The eyes were cool, almost cold, and her unpainted mouth had a faintly disdainful curl to it—the expressions of a member of the so-called upper class when dealing with someone far down in the pecking order. You wouldn't call her beautiful, but her figure was good and she was attractive enough if you liked them chilly and arrogant.

"My name is Ariana Quayles," she said. The words were clipped, the accent very properly British. "Mr. Martin Quayles's daughter."

"Oh, I see. I'm pleased to—"

She didn't let me finish it. "I should like to know why you're here instead of at the Prinsep Hotel. I do not appreciate shuttling about the city, and I am not in the habit of acting as a porter for an employee's luggage."

"Well," I said, "I'm sorry if I inconvenienced you. I've had some problems . . ."

"I'm sure." She couldn't have cared less about whatever problems I might have had; she'd only wanted to make sure I understood my place. The one hand came up and replaced the sunglasses, as though establishing a tangible barrier. "Come along, Mr. Connell. We've a rather long drive, you know."

She put her back to me and started over to the jeep. I stared after her briefly, with mounting irritation of my own: if she was her father's daughter, as they say, I didn't figure to last very long on the Union Jack. But then, I thought, I *had* put her through a little trouble on my behalf, and maybe my somber mood was causing me to overreact. I shrugged away the irascibility and followed her to the jeep and got in beside her. She gave me just enough time to close the door before she pulled us out into traffic.

As we passed through the city, I made an attempt at polite conversation. "Do you live with your father on the Union Jack, Miss Quayles?"

She glanced at me briefly, in a way that said she considered the question silly. "Of course."

"Then you help him in its operation?"

"I do."

"It must be a demanding job, running a rubber estate."

"One could say that."

"Do you get into K.L. often?"

"Mmm."

"It's a fine city. I used to live here, years ago."

"Did you."

Bored and monosyllabic responses—but I had the feeling that if I continued to ask questions, innocent as they were, she would make a point to remind me again of my place. I lapsed into silence. So much for polite conversation.

We drove north out of Kuala Lumpur along a good

two-lane road. Flooded rice paddies flanked it for a time, then gave way to forestland and the inevitable rubber plantations. Malay tappers worked among the trees: adding fresh cuts to naked, spirally striped trunks that had the look of monochromatic barber poles, affixing metal latex cups to yesterday's recut wounds. The leafy branches of the trees partially obscured the sun's glare, dappling the landscape with light and shadow.

Near the village of Kuang, we passed a huge tin dredge—mounds of tailings rising up like miniature mountains behind a cluster of work buildings—and then swung northeast toward the coast. Neither of us spoke further. Miss Quayles kept her eyes to the front, ignoring me, and I sat working on cigarettes and brooding about the past two days. She was a competent driver, if a little inclined toward excessive speed and indiscriminate use of the horn; we were making pretty good time.

Flat, grassy *padangs* replaced the rubber trees as the road hooked to parallel a small river. On both sides of the water were native *kampongs* built on stilts, and the road was lined with clattering wagons and children and dogs and pajama-clad old men. After a time we crossed a single-track rail line and came into the village of Batang Berjunta, on the Sungei Selangor. Beyond and to the east, then, I could see the beginnings of thick rain forest rising toward and over higher mountains, where Cameron Highlands, one of Malaya's wealthy resorts, was located. The jungle shone a hazy blackish-green against a deep indigo sky.

Once we came off the bridge spanning the river, the road ran straight as a taut piece of string toward the rain forest. But when we reached the jungle's perimeter, it right-angled to the west as though it wanted no part of that high, tangled mass of green darkness. Some eight kilometers along, the entrance to a narrow asphalt jungle road appeared and Miss

Quayles turned off. Thick walls comprised of palms and tapangs and wild rubber began to close in on us.

She said abruptly, "Mr. Connell?"

I looked at her, and her mouth was thin and she was staring into the rear-vision mirror. "What is it?"

"I believe we're being followed."

"What?" I twisted on the seat. We were just starting into a turn, but I had a glimpse of a small light blue car—Japanese, maybe—several hundred yards behind us.

"I first noticed it in K.L.," she said, "and it has been with us ever since, making every turn we have, matching our speed. Do you recognize the auto?"

"No."

"Neither do I. Why should anyone be following us, Mr. Connell?"

Mutt and Jeff, I thought. Jesus Christ! But maybe not; maybe it was a local citizen who just happened to be going in the same direction we were. Except that I didn't believe worth a damn in that sort of coincidence.

I shook my head, not speaking.

"Well," Miss Quayles said, "whoever it is certainly couldn't be interested in *me*."

Not many people are going to be interested in you, lady, I thought, until you come down out of your ivory tower and thaw out a little. But I still didn't say anything. The road had begun to serpentine, and now we were into genuine primeval jungle. The huge branches of tapang trees interlaced with lianas and other vines overhead, blotting out all but tiny winking flashes of sunlight, giving the roadway the appearance of a tunnel. Birds screeched and monkeys chattered in the heavy, cathedral-like gloom. You could smell thick hot dampness and the faint alcoholic odor of decaying vegetation.

Looking back, I had another fleeting glimpse of the

trailing car. I couldn't tell if it was the same one I'd seen leaving the vicinity of Maria Velasquez's shack last night, though the size of it looked about right. *Was* it Mutt and Jeff? There was one way to find out. And if it was, I didn't want them following us to the Union Jack—or, worse, trying to overtake us now that we were off the more populated roadways.

I said, "How far is it to the estate?"

"Perhaps fifteen kilometers."

"On this road?"

"All but the last six kilometers, yes."

"So there's an intersection where this one ends."

"Of course."

"Does that second road fork in either direction?"

"In both, as it happens."

"Four possible routes, then."

"Yes."

"Which means we stand a chance of losing them."

She looked at me. "I imagine we do."

"If you're as accomplished a driver as I think you are, it might be a good idea if we tried it."

"You know who is in that auto, don't you?"

"Maybe," I admitted. "But it's a long story, and if that car does contain a certain two men, there isn't any time for lengthy explanations."

"As bad as all that?"

"As bad as all that. I'm sorry, Miss Quayles."

I expected her to be frightened, and angry, but instead a faint smile moved the corners of her mouth. "I suggest you take hold of something," she said, and snap-shifted into second and came down hard on the accelerator.

The jeep's engine whined, roared, and we skidded sharply into a turn; ran out of it sidewheeling and went into another one. She was hunched forward over the wheel, one hand gripping it and the other working the floor stick. Her eyes were bright. She had spirit under that icy exterior; you had to give her that much. I braced my feet, hanging onto the seat back, watching behind us. There was no sign of the little blue car.

With tires howling on the asphalt, she brought the jeep out of another curve and into a climbing straight stretch. She shifted smoothly into third, accelerating. As we neared the top of the rise, we were traveling at better than sixty.

Just before we crested I saw the little car fishtail out of the last curve—and it was moving as fast as we were.

Miss Quayles had seen it, too, in the rear-vision mirror. "They're chasing us," she said, but it was nothing more than a flat statement of fact. If the situation had instilled fear of any sort in her, she wasn't letting it show.

I said "Yeah" between my teeth, because now there wasn't any doubt in my mind that it was Mutt and Jeff back there. The K.L. police obviously hadn't picked them up last night—and one of them must have been planted inside the Prinsep this morning, close enough to overhear the day manager tell Miss Quayles I was waiting for her at the National Mosque. Then they'd simply followed her. I was a fool for underestimating them, I told myself angrily; I should damned well have found my own way to the Union Jack. But hindsight buys you nothing in this world; you can't replay the past.

The jeep bounced up over the rise, careened down the other side. When I turned to look at the road ahead of us, I saw a sharp left turn coming up and thought she was going too fast for that one. I jammed my feet hard against the floorboards. She braked at the last second, gearing down; the rear end slewed around and narrowly missed the bole of a tree, but she fought the wheel and got us on a point again. I let breath out sibilantly.

63

"They shan't catch us," she said. She seemed almost to be perversely enjoying herself. "Whoever your friends are, they shan't catch us."

Two more curves and then another straight run of maybe a thousand yards, slanting downhill. The jungle receded on our left, giving way to a small stream choked with debris that meandered parallel to the roadway, fifteen or twenty feet below its level. Giant emerald ferns and the huge, vine-festooned trunks of tapang trees made a solid wall of the far stream bank; the steep clay slope on my side was dotted with limestone rocks and staghorn ferns and coils of olive-colored thorn brush.

We'd gone seven or eight hundred yards before I saw the little blue car shimmy into view behind us. Gaining on them, I thought; they don't know the road, and that Japanese model of theirs doesn't have a jeep's maneuverability. If we don't run into trouble, like meeting another car on one of these blind curves, we'll lose them all right.

The jeep barreled out of the stretch, and again I could no longer see the little blue job. Jungle flashed by on our right and the stream continued to border the road on our left as we went through a series of quick curves, then a short run. Still no further glimpse of our pursuit.

I felt the jeep begin to slide into a new turn—and Miss Quayles said "Oh!" in alarm and I twisted my head to the front. Three big, mangy-looking dholes—vicious wild dogs that run in packs—had started onto the road ahead of us. She hit the horn, downshifted, touched the brake. The dholes scattered, but there was an impact along the right front fender and a sharp barking cry: we'd hit one of them. The jeep yawed, tires wailing. She turned into the skid, accelerating lightly, not using the brake at all now. We began to straighten out.

Christ, I thought, that was close.

And the right rear tire blew.

64

# 10

The grenade-like concussion of exploding rubber shook the jeep, and the wheel wrenched out of Miss Quayles's hand and the rear end snapped all the way around. I lunged instinctively toward the wheel, grabbed it, but there was nothing I could do. We spun once, like a top, green and black surroundings in a kaleidoscopic whirl. I caught the back of her head and pushed it down in my lap, bracing her body with my own, still hanging onto the wheel with my other hand; she struggled, but she didn't make a sound. The jeep heeled over dangerously, stayed upright and spun again. All I could think was, My God, we're dead if we turn over; we're dead.

We came out of the second spin skidding rear end foremost, at an angle toward the embankment on the west. I got my foot over and jammed it down futilely on the brake: the jeep's rear wheels left the road, went over the bank's edge. The front end tilted up and we slid down backward, metal ripping shrilly against the limestone boulders; but the rocks and the soft mud sucking at the tires and undercarriage helped to slow our momentum. Then the rear end jarred into the shallow stream, slamming my head painfully into the dash. A white blaze of light erupted and then receded behind my eyes. Shivering, the jeep rolled almost gently onto its side, splashing us with dank-smelling water, spilling me on top of Miss Quayles against the driver's door, so that she was half-submerged.

I caught the wheel again and heaved myself off of her, then pulled her head up out of the stream. Her eyes were glassy and she was coughing and panting, but she didn't seem to be hurt. I twisted out of the jeep, struggling to get my feet under me in the knee-deep water. When I had my balance, I took hold of both her arms and dragged her out from under the wheel and stood her up next to me.

I heard the sound of the little car and looked up at the road in time to see it draw abreast of where we were. The driver—it was the tall one, Jeff—stood on the brakes and brought the machine to a slewing stop. I swung Miss Quayles around and tugged her across the muddy bottom and out of the stream on the opposite bank.

One of them shouted in English as we scrambled up the bank, boots sliding on wet mats of lichen. At the top I looked back again and neither of them had guns out in their hands; but I remembered clearly enough the knives they'd wielded the night before, and I had no weapon at all. I saw them start down in the scarred path left by the jeep, and then I faced front again and took us forward into the jungle.

Symmetrical tree trunks—smooth and black, red and scaly, ghostly green, marbled and dappled—rose a hundred feet before they branched, like immense pillared bars in a nightmarish dungeon. The undergrowth was impossibly dense, a wavy sea of parasitic vines and seedling trees and great green leaves that hid most of the root networks and lower trunks of the tapangs; the earth itself was invisible beneath thick humus filmed with muddy slime. Lianas and creepers hung down from the branches high overhead and looped around the trees and one another. Hanging gardens of rotting mosses and ferns combined with the tightly woven canopy of the tapang leaves to completely obliterate the sky. Animal life teemed around us—creeping, climbing, burrowing—but the only thing I saw was a russet-brown, grizzle-faced orangutan tottering on bent knees through the branches like a high-wire walker under a circus dome.

You needed a *parang* knife to make any kind of decent headway through the surface growth, but I managed an erratic course by ripping at the vines and seedlings with my free hand. The air was saturated with heat, and the light had an unhealthy greenish tinge; the smell of fungus and decay was like that in a tomb, overpowering, nauseating. The jungle was every bit as frightening as I recalled it from brief experience two years before, when I had worked a rubber plantation in Ipoh. But above its blended noises I thought I could hear Mutt and Jeff tracking somewhere behind us, and right now they represented a greater menace than the surroundings.

Unseen birds and monkeys screeched at us from above; mosquitoes and other insects fed on our faces and arms. A fat black leech dropped off a leaf onto the web of skin between my left thumb and forefinger, but I managed to swipe it off before its suction disks could take hold. We stumbled over concealed roots, and the vines seemed to clutch at us like sentient fingers. Once my foot came down on something soft and brittle that had to be the newly dead corpse of some small jungle creature.

The undergrowth became so wildly tangled finally that I knew we couldn't penetrate it, didn't dare penetrate it. I stopped at the strangler fig-enwrapped bole of a tapang, pawing my eyes free of streaming sweat, and listened. Natural jungle sounds, nothing more. Some of the tenseness drained out of me, and I realized I was still tightly clutching Miss Quayles's arm. I released it, turning to her.

Her face and hair were wet from the stream water and from perspiration, and her breasts heaved with the irregular tempo of her breathing. There were dark red finger marks on her arm where I'd held her; she rubbed at the spot gingerly with the palm of her other hand. The gray-green eyes, looking into mine, contained anger and a hint of the same exhilaration I had seen in them during the high-speed road chase—and, for the first time, an undercurrent of fright.

I worked saliva through my dry mouth. "They won't find us now," I said. "I think they've given it up."

She took a long, shuddering breath, and I could see that she was beginning to regain some of her composure. She asked thickly, "Was it really necessary to come so far into the jungle to escape those men?"

"Yeah, it was necessary."

"Just who are they?"

"I don't know."

"Then why are they after you?"

"I don't know that either."

Her lips pursed slightly.

"I'm telling you the truth," I said.

"Are you in some sort of trouble with the authorities?"

"No."

A leech dropped suddenly onto her arm from above, but she didn't react the way most women would have. She just sliced it away as though it were only a mosquito. "You could have left me back at the jeep," she said. "I was a bit dazed and cumbersome, after all. Why did you take the time to carry me along?"

"Because, among other things, those men are murderers. They've killed two people that I know of, and one a woman. I'm not going to let them kill anybody else if I can help it."

She didn't change expression. "I see."

68

"Look, I'll give you the whole story—as much of it as I know—when we get out of here. I'm an innocent pawn in a sordid business I don't understand, which sounds trite and melodramatic but happens to be a fact nonetheless, and I'm damned sorry you had to get dragged into it too. I wouldn't blame you in the least if you sent me packing; I seem to have become a harbinger of trouble the past two days."

"That sounds rather like self-pity."

"Maybe it is, a little. If so, it's not unwarranted."

Her eyes studied me, and I couldn't read them at all now; she was in full control again. And yet I had the feeling that the cool superiority had been replaced not with apprehension or distrust or antipathy, as you might expect, but with curiosity and something else less definable. In any case, I was no longer someone to be ignored or discounted.

At length she smiled grimly and said, "Well, we shall worry about those men later on. At the moment we've another problem."

"What problem?"

"Just how well do you know the jungle?"

"Not very. Why?"

"I've lived near it all my life," she said. "It's quite like a maze, you know. You enter it and you think you can step right out again whenever you choose; but when you do look about for the exit, it isn't at all where you expected it to be."

I stared at her.

"Which means, Mr. Connell, we might very possibly be lost."

"Lost? We haven't come that far."

"Ten meters is far enough in the jungle."

"We can backtrail."

"Can we, really?"

I turned and looked back the way we had come—what I'd thought but was suddenly not at all certain was the way we had come. The jungle growth was incredibly dense and dark and chaotic: like a maze, all right, like a maze far more complex than any which could be devised by the human mind. And I remembered an old Tamil telling me once, in Ipoh, that nearly every person's built-in compass ceases to function in a Malaysian rain forest; and that people have gotten lost after entering the jungle by only a few yards, while other people trapped for days or weeks have finally been found dead the same distance from roads or rubber estates or native villages.

Miss Quayles was still watching me. "Rather an unpleasant prospect, isn't it?"

I didn't say anything.

"It's as much my fault as yours, I suppose, although I was a bit groggy. Perhaps those two men know the jungle, too, and that's why they gave up the chase."

"Yeah," I said bitterly.

"Shall we stay here awhile longer?"

"No. If they got back to the road, they're not going to hang around for long; somebody's bound to come along sooner or later, and they're not going to want to answer any questions about the jeep. One thing's sure, though: they'll check the jeep's registration before they leave. And then they'll know about the Union Jack."

Apprehension flickered finally in her eyes, and I thought that it was likely concern for her father; she had normal filial emotions, at least. "They won't approach it directly?" she said.

There was no telling what a pair like Mutt and Jeff might do, but I didn't want to give her anything to worry about along those lines. "I doubt it. But they'll be around, watching and waiting. The thing we've got to do is contact your father as soon as we can."

"Yes," she said. "As soon as we can."

I started to take her hand, thought better of it, and moved

back through the tangled green labyrinth. "We'll find the road," I said over my shoulder. "We'll find it."

But I was wrong: we didn't.

We were lost, all right—damned good and lost.

# 11

After half an hour, maybe longer, we gave up the futile search for the road—for the moment, anyway—and paused in what passed for a tiny jungle glade. Red stinging ants had gotten into my clothing, and so had a couple of leeches. There were sore areas on my legs and neck and even on one instep, where one of the filthy things had gotten through a boot eyehole and sunk into my flesh through the sock. I tried not to think about the true stories I had heard of humans occasionally dying when leeches—or the swelling caused by a surfeit of their bites—blocked anal and other body orifices.

What I did keep focused in my mind was something else the old Tamil in Ipoh had told me about the Malaysian jungles. There is nothing in them, except seldom seen wild buffalo, which is really and overtly dangerous to man; even tigers and snakes and elephants will go out of their way to avoid contact with humans. The true threat to any lost individual comes from within himself: inbred fear of the wilderness, a kind of creeping claustrophobia, terror of the strange and unknown, foolish actions born of panic. Imagination, he'd said, had killed more lost men than the jungle alone ever would.

Miss Quayles knew that too, obviously. She had visible leech bites on one arm and both hands, and mosquito swellings on her left cheekbone, but she'd endured all of that as well as the frustration without complaint or comment. She was an odd one in a lot of ways, but beneath the seemingly shallow exterior there were strength and character and an intricate depth which I couldn't fathom.

I got out my cigarettes and lit two and gave one to her. I said then, "How large is this stretch of jungle?"

"Quite large. North-south, it extends from the main road we were on earlier to the lower perimeter of our estate; and to the west, with the exception of a few smallholdings and an abandoned tin dredge, it reaches all the way to the coast."

"Would there be any other roads or trails nearby?"

"Native and elephant trails, of course, but nothing else in this vicinity. A narrow tributary of the Bernam, the Sungei Kerling, winds from northeast to southwest, through the Union Jack, and eventually empties into the Strait. On the river, perhaps two or three kilometers northwest of where we are now, there is a Sakai village. Senoi, actually."

"Sakai" is a generic term contemptuously given by the Malays, and used generally by most inhabitants of Malaysia, to a variety of pygmyish aboriginal tribes like the Senoi and Semang. It means "slave-people." Persecuted, vanishing breeds of primitive man, they lived in crude villages or deeper in the jungle in caves, like animals. They feared all other races, and they feared and worshipped the *rimau* or jungle tiger; they could swing through the trees like apes, could and did eat anything dead or growing in the earth. Blowguns and *parang*-type knives were their weapons, but they weren't actively hostile and we had nothing to be afraid of if we made contact.

I said, "Well, we've got two alternatives. We can stay right here and wait until somebody finds the jeep and your father organizes a search, or we can try to get out on our own. We've still got to be fairly close to the road, and that's a point in our favor either way. We might get ourselves even more lost by moving around, but then there's no guarantee that searchers could find us no matter what we do. Personally, I don't like the idea of standing around waiting for help from other people, and particularly not in a place like this jungle."

"I agree," Miss Quayles said. "We've only to locate the road or the river or a trail, and it seems hopeful we'll eventually come upon one or another by mucking about."

I dropped the butt of my cigarette into a puddle of green-slimed water. "Ready, then?"

"Ready, Mr. Connell."

We set out again, struggling around and through the chaotic network of vines and young palms and seedlings and immense tapangs. The pervading alcoholic smell of rotting humus had made my stomach queasy, and I was careful to breathe only through my mouth. The jungle sounds were constant and diverse—the sweet, chuckling laugh of gibbons, the buzzing of bees and insects, the calls of hornbills and other birds, the booming cry of a siamang, half a hundred others that I couldn't identify; but except for an occasional glimpse of a monkey or a flying squirrel or a bright-winged bird, its inhabitants remained invisible.

It was impossible to move in a straight line. All you could do was to take whatever openings you could find, and then part of the time you would come up against an impenetrable barrier of vegetation and have to backtrack and alter course to compensate. One of those barriers was a wide section of man-high lalang grass that forced us to change direction entirely. Lalang of that type can cut a human to ribbons if he tries to pass through it; rigid and slashing, the blades of grass are more like the blades of thin, sharp knives.

74

We kept moving without pause, because the maddening slowness of our pace made rest stops unnecessary. Rattans and other thorns, some with needles like long, hooked scimitars, seemed to sprout in thick tangles at every turn, further impeding our progress. I was soaked with sweat; we seldom saw the sky and never the sun, but heat came up from the jungle floor in near-tangible waves. The leeches and mosquitoes were merciless.

We didn't find the road, or anything resembling a native or elephant trail.

Some of the watery light began at length to fade, creating shadows that appeared to crouch behind tree trunks and giant ferns. I sleeved my stinging eyes clear of wetness and looked at my watch: just four o'clock. It seemed as if we had been in that green hell for an endless string of hours, instead of for less than three.

A low rumbling sound echoed suddenly from beyond the massive knitted canopy above, unmistakable in origin. It was thunder, presaging as usual one of Southeast Asia's frequent late afternoon rains. Fine, I thought sardonically, that's all we need now. I glanced at Miss Quayles, and we stopped without speaking and looked up and listened. The drum rolls of thunder deepened, grew closer together. In tacit agreement we moved beneath a young, thick-fronded palm.

When it came, the cloudburst was torrential. The sound of the rain hitting the dome of leaves and branches seemed almost deafening; if we had had anything to say to each other, we would have had to shout to make ourselves heard. Monkeys scurried unseen through the greenery, seeking shelter. Water filtered down in droplets and string-thin cascades, dripped warmly onto us through the palm fronds, glistened jewel-like on vines and leaves in the semi-gloom.

The rain pelted down for twenty minutes or more, abated slightly, and then stopped altogether. But the trees continued to drip water in a soft, steady, maddening pulse of sound, like a million leaky faucets. The downpour, and the coming of night, had lessened the stifling heat and created coolness in the heavy air; but it was a damp and clammy coolness: one discomfort exchanged for another. The encroaching shadows had begun to deepen and lengthen rapidly now. We had maybe half an hour before full darkness settled within the jungle.

I mentioned that to Miss Quayles, and she nodded. "We'd better find a place to spend the night," I said then. "We're not going to find a way out of here until sometime early tomorrow, the way it looks."

The faint smile curved the corners of her mouth again. "You're an optimistic man, aren't you?"

"Sometimes," I said. "Pessimism has its place, but this isn't it. Or don't you think so, Miss Quayles?"

"Yes, I suppose I do. The desire for self-preservation inspires optimism, doesn't it?" She paused, looking at me steadily. "You may call me Ariana, if you like."

She was a strange woman, all right. And a fascinating one, too. I hadn't really been aware of her physically since I had first seen her in K.L.— and when the awareness came in that moment, I realized that despite or maybe because of the present circumstances, she was damned attractive. The damp dishevelment of her hair, the flush of exertion in her cheeks, the absence of the cool arrogance all combined to give her a soft, strongly compelling allure. I found myself noticing, as well, the way the wet green jacket clung to her breasts, outlining her bra and the faint turgidity of buttonlike nipples, and the way her slacks pulled into a tight divided V at the apex of her legs. Irrationally, I felt a sudden faint stirring of sexual desire. I had not had a woman in some time, and I had not had a woman like Ariana Quayles in a very long time . . .

I looked away from her and shook myself mentally and thought: For Christ's sake, Connell! I said sharply, "Okay, you're Ariana and I'm Dan. Now we'd better move before it gets any darker."

"Just as you say—Dan."

I thought there might have been a touch of amusement in the way she said that, but when I glanced at her once more the faint smile was gone and her face was perfectly serious.

We fought our way silently through the wet undergrowth for maybe fifteen minutes, and came then into another tiny clearing—this one dotted with moss-shawled limestone rocks. It was as good a place as any. There was very little light left, and stars shone in what sky was visible here.

Miss Quayles—Ariana—said, "The natives build primitive fireplaces by interweaving vines and branches and covering the whole with mud; I expect we can do the same. We really ought to have a fire."

"Agreed."

I cleared a space in the center of the clearing, watching for reptiles and colonies of red and black jungle ants; there were none. Then we gathered vines and sturdy dead wood, dug up as much fairly dry fuel as we could find beneath the layers of humus, snapped off palm fronds to make a bed. Our throats were parched with thirst and we paused to drink fresh rainwater that had collected in the cuplike leaves of small, furry, gray-green plants. It was too late to think about hunting up such food as the jungle offered—bananas, coconuts, wild brinjals—but for the moment hunger was the least of our problems.

The last of the daylight vanished while we worked. With the advent of full darkness, the normal daytime clamor decreased until, momentarily, a thick hush fell over the forest. Then, with startling abruptness, new and different sounds burst violently all around us. Thousands of cicadas combined in a sonorous symphony, and toads and frogs croaked a loud baritone accompaniment. Bats screamed and chattered like fishwives over durian and other fruit, their wings beating the air in a kind of leathery cadence. A prowling tiger made a peculiar moaning, snoring call some distance away, seeking to flush a sambar or *plandok* deer. These and myriad other sounds swelled, ebbed to silence, swelled again in a way that made my neck cold. The old Tamil had been right about a man's imagination; I had to make a concentrated effort to keep mine under control.

When we finished constructing the fireplace—two feet high and crudely conical-shaped, overlaid with slimy earth—I arranged the wood fuel inside the hood and then touched it off with a match. Billows of acrid smoke poured outward, but the flame died almost immediately. It took me several minutes to get a steady, still smoky fire burning.

We laid out the palm fronds in front of the fire, then sat on them cross-legged, side by side, and worked on cigarettes and thought our own thoughts. The fire put out some heat, but not enough to dry our clothing or dull the edge of the night's gathering chill. Flickering brightly, the flames cast weird shadows against the dark, alien background of the jungle. The play of red-orange light on Ariana's face made her seem very young and very vulnerable—and yet, ambivalently, added a mystical aura, an atavistic sensuality, to her as a woman.

I had an urge to put my arm around her, draw her near. Man, the lusty and dominant, the protector; woman, the passive and weak, the protected. Bullshit. So I sat there without moving, feeling all at once tired and empty and foolish and lonely—and thought for the first time in years of the girl in San Francisco, and of what life might have been like if she had kept her fervent promise long ago to wait for me no matter what.

# 12

It was a long while before either of us spoke again. Ariana bent forward and unlaced her right boot and took it and her stocking off. A thickly bloated leech had gotten through both and fastened itself to the skin between two of her toes. She pressed the burning end of her cigarette against it, and it shriveled instantly and fell away. She put the stocking and boot back on.

I heaped more fuel on the fire. When I settled back again, she broke the stillness between us finally by saying, "I should think it was time you told me about those two men."

"All right." Encapsulating, but omitting nothing important, I related the events of the past two days. She listened without interruption, her body half-turned toward me now, left knee almost touching mine. Her face was impassive, one side in darkness and the other side hellishly rouged by the dancing firelight—like a symbolic theological mask.

She said when I was finished, "You have had a rather bad time of it, haven't you?"

"Not as bad as Kirby or Maria Velasquez."

"You've no idea at all what the Red Fire might be?"

"None. Except that it has to be fairly small, something a man can carry around on his person or in his luggage."

"Mightn't it be a precious gem, such as a blood ruby?"

"Maybe. I hadn't thought of that possibility. Whatever it is, it's a hell of a lot more valuable to them than human life."

She extended her hands toward the fire; it had gotten very cold now. In a different voice, the one edged with concern, she said, "You really don't believe there's a chance they've . . . approached my father?"

"No—particularly not if he's called in the authorities to help search for you. It's me they're after; no one else."

"We'll have to go to the police when we've gotten out of here, you know."

"I know. Why do you say it like that?"

"Well, you've just told me you called them anonymously in K.L., after the girl's death."

"And you're wondering why I didn't give my name."

"Yes. And why you didn't go in person."

"I couldn't tell them anything more face to face than I did over the phone. Besides, I didn't feel like making myself a prime suspect in a murder case, which is exactly what I would have been since they didn't turn up Mutt and Jeff."

"You'll look even more guilty now, won't you."

I held her eyes with mine. "Do the police have to know that part of it?"

"Perhaps not. If you tell me why else you didn't go to them—what you're holding back."

"What makes you think I'm holding anything back?"

"You are, aren't you?"

I hesitated. "Okay," I said at length, "you'd find out about it sooner or later, because the police will, once they've run a routine check into my background." I leaned forward to toss more wood onto the fire, pulled the chill wet cloth of my bush jacket away from my skin. "The fact is, I've got a not very pretty past. Up until three years ago I was a smuggler, disguised as a commercial freight pilot operating out of K.L. and then Singapore. At one time or another since the end of the Korean conflict, I ferried anything you can name except drugs and human beings."

She didn't say anything for a moment, her face still impassive. But when she spoke again there was a trace of fascination in her voice: "I shouldn't think smuggling is such a terrible business."

"A lot of people wouldn't; it's been romanticized all out of proportion. In reality it happens to be one of the cheapest, dirtiest ways of earning the fast dollar. Ask any cop in the world about smuggling. He'll tell you the same thing."

"You couldn't have thought that while you were doing it."

"No. I didn't think about it much at all. It was the money I was concerned with, always the money and what I could buy with it."

"What changed your mind?" she asked. "What happened three years ago?"

"I was responsible for the death of my best friend, the only real friend I've ever had." And I told her the whole story of Pete Falco, the way it had been that flaming night on Penang. It was the first time I had talked about it in detail to anyone, and the telling was not as painful as I might have thought. That shallow grave I'd dug in the corner of my mind was deeper than I realized.

Ariana said, "And after that you quit smuggling altogether."

"That's right."

"Only because of what happened to your friend?"

"Yes. I could have gone back into it without much trouble, even with the government pressure; not in Singapore, maybe, but just about anywhere else in Southeast Asia. Money just stopped being important, and the life I had been leading became meaningless and distasteful. Some people find that hard to understand, and so they don't believe it. I guess I won't blame you if you're one of them."

"I believe you," she said—and I felt that she meant it.

There was an abrupt rustling sound in the canopy behind us, and then a fluttering swish of air. A large black shape with a full four-foot wing span and bright yellow, night-wide eyes swooped down overhead, vanished again into the foliage on the far side of the glade.

"Flying lemur," Ariana said. "Strange creatures, but harmless."

"It's too bad you can't say exactly the same about man."

That got me her faint smile again. Then she looked into the fire and said, "What have you done these three years, Dan?"

"Coolie labor on the Singapore River, mostly. Good, clean, honest work, if not particularly satisfying."

"Is a need for satisfaction the reason you've come to the Union Jack?"

"Partially. I guess I'm looking for a niche, too, something substantial—the kind of job that offers commitment and allows for peace of mind."

"I see."

"The only trouble is," I said wryly, "I seem to have acquired a knack for getting myself involved in other people's intrigues, like with Mutt and Jeff. Maybe it's a kind of added punishment for my sins." One of my legs had gone to sleep, and I stretched it out to one side of the crude fireplace. "I don't suppose your father will want me working for him when he learns the truth about me."

"I shouldn't worry about that. He's a reasonable man."

"I'm glad to hear that," I said. "All I want is a chance to prove myself."

She looked at me again. "Oddly enough, he once told me he'd said that very same thing to my mother in 1946. He was in Malaya during the Second World War, with the Argylls, and when he returned home to England, Mother wanted him to take a position with her dad's brokerage firm. He'd become smitten with Malaya and was quite determined to make a career as a planter. Mother relented, of course, and got her dad to finance them when they came out."

She seemed to have finally opened up a little, maybe because of my own personal candor, and I was beginning to almost like her as well as covet her. She was still a complicated entity, with facets of personality that were less than endearing, but I had the feeling now that basically she wasn't at all the type of cold bitch I had first decided she was. And I wanted to know more about her, as much as she was willing to reveal.

Too, talking the way we were now helped to keep both our minds off the position we were in.

I said, "You were born here, then?"

"Yes. Mother never took to the area the way Father did, particularly when the Communist guerrillas began making a nightmare of plantation life, and when I was old enough she insisted I be sent to London for schooling. I couldn't wait to come home during summer holidays. She was a wonderful woman, but she never quite understood Father and me."

"Was?"

"She died when I was eleven. Just before it happened, when she knew she wouldn't get well, she made my father promise to bury her in England. He hated the idea, but of course he kept his promise. He returns to London every year to visit her grave."

"And he's never remarried?"

"My mother was the only woman in his life; no one could even come close to replacing her. Since her death, he's devoted himself to the estate—and to me, I suppose."

I nodded; there was nothing I could say to that.

Ariana said, "I expect at the moment he's frantic with

worry. He's quite good in crises, except when they concern me."

"We'll be out of here tomorrow."

"For his sake, I hope so." She slapped ineffectually at the relentless swarms of mosquitoes. "You know, you and he have a bit in common."

"In what way?"

"You're both rather stubborn and strong-willed, for one. And, ironically, Father happens to be a flying enthusiast. He bought his own plane a number of years ago, and built an airstrip on the estate. He flies regularly to Singapore and Bangkok, among other places."

"Do you fly too?"

"No. Father thinks it's exhilarating—man and machine alone in the heavens, looking down on the world—but I prefer the solid earth."

"I used to feel the way he does," I said. "Not anymore. Since the crash on Penang I haven't gone near a plane; I never want to go up in one again. Just the thought of flying makes my nerves jump."

"Yes, I can imagine."

She stared into the fire again, and silence built up again between us. Fatigue had ended her desire for conversation, and mine as well. After a time I said, "We'd better try to sleep now. We're going to need all the rest we can get for tomorrow."

She nodded, and I fed the last of the fuel into the fire—making it blaze, at least momentarily, bright and hot. Ariana uncrossed her legs, turned on her buttocks and then stretched out on her back with her head toward the fire. I joined her and we covered ourselves with the fronds and lay there side by side, not touching, not speaking. A parrot screeched, and I could hear the night beasts prowling in search of animate and inanimate food. The darkness beyond the reach of the firelight was as thick as ink.

With nothing else to consume, the fire began to bank—and cold settled over us like a blanket of thin ice. Ariana said, "Dan."

"Yeah?"

There was a pause, and then, softly but with faint challenge: "We'd be warmer if we held each other, wouldn't we?"

I turned my head to look at her, and she was hugging herself and shivering visibly. Her face was expressionless. Without saying anything I extended my arm toward her, and she slid over and pillowed her head on my shoulder, body fitting against my right side. She lay rigidly. I rearranged the fronds over us, folded my arms around her. I could smell the faintness of perfume about her, a good musky female odor that even the presence of dried sweat failed to taint.

I said, "All right?"

"Yes."

There was no real intimacy in our embrace; and yet I was acutely aware of the feel of her body, the pressure of her breasts, the flat hardness of her stomach, the supple strength in her legs—and I thought that the palpable beat of her heart was more rapid than it should have been. I wanted to lift her head and kiss her, but I didn't think she would want it—at least not here, tonight. I kept my hands still on her back.

We lay that way for a long while. Then the tempo of her breathing became regular, and she relaxed against me, snuggling the way a woman does against a man in sleep. I held her more tightly, my face pressed to the silkiness of her hair.

The last thing I remember hearing was the wild laugh of a monkey, as though it had been watching us and was vastly amused at the foolish antics of the pair of *Homo sapiens* trapped in its world. . . .

# 13

The commencing and blended day sounds of the jungle woke us at the first light. It was still penetratingly cold, and we were still wet and badly chilled and covered with mosquito welts and purplish leech bites and thin networks of cuts and thorn scratches; but at least it hadn't rained again. We had little to say to each other, but that had nothing to do with the way we had passed the night. The relationship which had developed between us was one you couldn't easily define. I had no real idea just what sort of feelings she might have for me, and my own feelings for her were nebulous. All I knew for sure, after having held her as I had, was that I wanted to make love to her more than I had wanted to make love to a woman in a decade or more, and that when the time and place were right, I would find out for certain if she had any of the same desires.

We drank of, then washed gingerly with, water held by the leaves of the furry gray-green plants. Hunger began to gnaw demandingly under my breastbone as we started forward again through the endless sea of trees and undergrowth. Finding food was a primary consideration now.

We turned up nothing for a time, but then we came on a patch of jungle bamboo and Ariana said, "There are edible kernels at the roots of this type of bamboo. At least, I believe it's this type."

"We'll find out soon enough." I dropped to my knees and used my penknife to expose the roots of the outer stalks: she was right. I gathered up a handful of the large kernels and we peeled off the outer skins; they were sweet and nutty, if not very substantial. I dug more and put those into my pockets, and we pushed forward again.

A few minutes later Ariana noticed a wild coconut palm with nuts lying strewn at its base. Most were rotten and odorous, but we picked up three that looked all right. I broke one open, spilling only a little of the milk, and we drank that and ate the meat. Bamboo kernels and coconuts—some feast. Except that in a way it was; it was just fine, because it chased the pangs of hunger and seemed to give us both a feeling of renewed strength.

We went on. And on. And on. It grew warm, and then hot, and we traded back again the one form of discomfort for the other. Patches of blue sky and occasional crimson or purple orchids half-hidden among the upper tree branches were the only touches of color in the dank, dark greenness. Gibbons swung overhead at great speed, and an animal that was probably a tapir lumbered noisily nearby in a flash of black and dull white. We saw a monitor lizard as long as my arm, and a swarm of bees around a slender, sacklike honeycomb, and a python twenty feet in length hanging by its tail from a branch high above, body immobile against a speckled trunk; but we didn't see anything that pointed the way out.

I stopped fighting the renewed assault of the leeches—unlike the mosquitoes, they're inactive during the dark hours—and unless one of them threatened a tender part of my body,

I let them feed until they were gorged into tiny balloons. You couldn't feel them sucking your blood; it was only afterward that the soreness developed. I tried to keep my mind blank, but that was like trying not to sweat. So I thought of a cold mineral bath, and iced Anchor beer, and spicy Malay food, and a bed in a well-lighted and air-conditioned room—and of the trails and roads and rivers that had to be all around us. I kept telling myself we were traveling in roughly one direction, that we were not merely wandering in hopeless circles.

The heat gained full intensity, and the rank smell increased until the air was almost suffocating. Mid-morning. Mosquitoes and leeches. Lianas like the riggings of disintegrated shipwrecks sunken beneath green, dark water. Sweat, stinging ants, thorns. Noon. Fresh water to appease growing thirst. Clothes still damp and clammy, chafing inner thighs, creating painful rashes. We found a wild banana tree and ate two green bananas each and smoked the last two cigarettes in my pack. Early afternoon. Giant ferns with stems that cut thinly, agonizingly into flesh. Another disinterested python. Leeches and mosquitoes. Ariana got her foot caught in the foliage-hidden stilt roots of a pandanus tree, and twisted the ankle, but not so badly that she was unable to walk without my help. Mid-afternoon. A brief deluge of rain, soaking us anew. The distant trumpeting of an elephant, directionless. Tapangs and palms and kapurs and screw pines, vines and ferns and bracken and thorns. Stifling air. Odor. Decay. Mosquitoes and leeches . . .

The terrain began to slope steadily downward, and the undergrowth shared the earth with mossy limestone outcroppings. A deep ravine loomed off on our left, choked with an impenetrable mass of vegetation that the Malays call *belukar:* a secondary jungle which forms after part of the primitive forest has been momentarily cleared by man or nature.

Visible in wide sections here, the sky was hazy with shimmering heat.

Ariana said my name, and I stopped immediately. She was breathing heavily, and her swollen features were sheened with sweat. The way she stood, shifting her weight from one side to the other, told me the muscles in her legs were as tight and sore as my own.

"How's your ankle?" I asked her.

"Well enough, except for twinges."

"We'll rest here for a while."

"Yes." She stared down into the ravine, and then transferred her gaze to the sloping line of jungle beyond it and to our right. Almost to herself, then, she said, "The river lies just above sea level."

"What?"

She turned to me. "It's possible we're heading west. Elevations north and south vary from two to two hundred and fifty meters, and the land is fairly flat. But to the west, not far from the Sungei Kerling, it drops steadily; the river, as I said, lies just above sea level."

"You're sure of this?"

"I've lived in this area all my life, and I've had occasion to study the relief charts my father keeps in his plane. But I'm not certain we *are* heading west, of course."

"Let's hope we are," I said grimly. "Let's damn well hope so."

We rested for five minutes, and then we set out to skirt the rim of the ravine: climbing over the damp, slippery rock, still descending. There were no more outcroppings then, and the mass of jungle, the tangle of lianas grew thicker. We struggled through layers of rotting humus more than a foot in depth, undisturbed for centuries, untouched until that moment by the step of civilized or primitive man. I had a sudden, eerie feeling of displacement in time, as though with each step we were traveling backward across the eons.

The terrain seemed to level off finally, and the labyrinth of vegetation became so complex that movement in any direction brought us up against near-impassable obstructions. I ripped viciously at a web of lianas in a release of pentup frustration, cursing in a steady, vomitlike outpouring of words. Breath rattled in my throat, ached in my lungs, and finally forced me to cut off the string of invective. When I looked then at Ariana I saw that she was standing motionless, watching me without expression. There was a small leech pulsing faintly on the side of her neck.

I stepped up to her and ripped the thing loose and flung it down. She didn't move. My face was inches from hers, and our eyes locked; we stood that way. I could feel weakness down low in my belly, and when the tip of her tongue came out to moisten her cracked lips I knew she wanted me to kiss her as much as I wanted it: not in passion but in a need for closeness and contact, two people lost and desperately wanting a tangible fusion of the flagging strength and hope of each. I brought my hands up and took her shoulders.

And suddenly, from off to our left and not far away, there was a bellowing animal sound.

Our heads twisted automatically in that direction, breaking the spell of the moment. The sound came again. I looked at Ariana, and her mouth trembled and her eyes had grown bright. "Crocodile!" she said. "Dan, that's a bloody lovely bull crocodile!"

"The river," I said.

"Yes, yes, the river. We can't be more than a few meters from it."

We stood looking at each other for two or three heartbeats, and then we turned together and began tearing frenziedly at the undergrowth. The bull croc roared again, closer; we had to be almost there. I thought I could smell the river then, the rank wet intoxicating odor of moving water, and I was like an animal myself those last few yards: hands turned into ripping claws, feet into slashing hoofs.

I saw it: a flash of rippling brown through the vegetation.

And then we broke all the way through, onto a slender swatch of mud three feet above the slow-moving water.

"Dan," she said, "oh, Dan," and came up against me. We clung to each other, looking out at the most beautiful damned ugly brown debris-ridden river in all of Southeast Asia.

It was maybe seventy-five yards wide at this point, walled by the jungle as far as you could see in both directions. To our left, south, and several hundred yards distant, was a sharp westward bend; to our right it ran straight as a stretched ribbon. The bull crocodile we had heard was lying on a tiny mud island in close to the near bank, and the heads of two others were visible above the river's surface—savage throwbacks to prehistoric days. The sky overhead was a sweet, hazy blue.

Ariana and I broke apart finally, but her hand found mine and held it tightly. I said, "Have you got any idea where we are?" in a voice thickened by relief.

"I think so. That bend should be the final one before a two-kilometer straight. I can't recall another lengthy straight like this one."

"If you're right, how far are we from that Senoi village?"

"It's located along the first bend at the end of the straight."

"Upriver from here, then. A couple of kilometers."

"Yes."

"We can't get there by following the bank," I said. "It's too overgrown, and if we have to move away from the river, we run the risk of losing ourselves again." I looked out at the crocodiles. The bull had moved around on its squat legs; with its tail swaying from side to side, it seemed to be staring back at me out of huge reptilian eyes. "And we can't swim for it, either."

"Mightn't we fashion a raft?"

"Bamboo stalks, maybe, lashed together with vines: yeah. We'd have to pole against the current, but it doesn't seem strong. We ought to be able to make two kilometers, if the raft holds together and it doesn't rain again and the crocodiles leave us alone."

I looked at my watch, and it was just four o'clock. "We'd better hurry. It'll be dusk in another couple of hours."

There was a line of young bamboo, some of the stalks four and five inches in diameter, off on our right. We plowed to it through the undergrowth, and I used my knife to cut off ten of the thicker, more resilient pieces down close to the ground. Then I sliced off several of the stronger looking vines. While Ariana stripped the vines of leaves, I trimmed the bamboo into six-foot lengths.

I said then, "How deep is the river, do you have any idea?"

"No more than a couple of meters, I'm sure."

"Ten-foot poles ought to do it, if we stay in as close to the bank as possible."

I cut two of those, two inches in diameter, and trimmed them. Working one at either end, and then together in the middle, we lashed the stalks together to form the raft; tied off the vine ropes. It was slow, arduous work, and the whole operation took us better than an hour and a half. The color of the sky had modulated to dusky gray, and the beginnings of the evening hush had fallen over the rain forest, before we were satisfied that the raft was as sturdy as we could make it.

We dragged it to the river's edge and I slid it down into the water, holding onto it to keep it from drifting. The bull croc still watched from the mud island, and the other two were looking in our direction as well; but they weren't interested enough to come investigating—at least not yet.

When I lifted myself up and onto the raft, water lapped over the edges and came up through the stalks. But it held my weight all right. I caught one of the network of hanging lianas, motioned to Ariana to hand me the navigation poles. Once she had done that I helped her on top beside me; it took her weight, too, without buckling.

"We'll have to pole from a kneeling position," I said. "We don't dare take the chance of standing up."

She nodded.

"Okay. Set?"

"Set."

Kneeling side by side, legs and hips touching, we took up the poles. I dipped mine into the shallow water at the bank and shoved us out away from the overhanging vegetation. The crocodiles remained where they were. The current was sluggish enough, but it gave us a little trouble at first, until we managed to synchronize our poling. Ariana was a strong girl, and she put good muscle into her end of it. We began to make headway, slowly but steadily.

After a time we drew abreast of a narrow spit of mud with four more big, brown-slimed crocs on it. One of them slid off and into the water, and uneasily I watched it come out toward us. I nudged Ariana, pointing. We both lifted our poles out of the river, and I held mine upraised like a club; but when the thing was ten feet from the raft it decided it didn't want to bother with us after all, and veered off and kept on gliding toward the opposite bank. I released the breath I had been holding, and we dug in again with the poles.

Illumination began to fade from the sky; we had no more than a few minutes, I thought, before full dark. The cicadas and toads and frogs started up in the blackening jungle. I stared down the dusky ribbon of the river, but there was still no sign of the Senoi village—no light of any kind, no break in the thick forest wall. It was impossible to tell exactly how far

93

we had come from our commencement point, though when I looked back downriver I couldn't see the bend at all. More than a kilometer, maybe. At least that.

The raft seemed to be holding up: I could detect no loosening or unraveling of the vine ropes. Ariana and I were in a less sound shape. Weakened by the multitude of parasite bites and the long, grueling trek through the jungle, both of us were functioning on slim reserves of stamina. The muscles in my neck and chest and arms ached painfully from the constant strain of poling; and as able-bodied as Ariana was, I could see by the increasing effort with which she dipped the length of bamboo into the water, by the grimace on her face, that she was nearing the limit of her endurance. But we couldn't give in now, not this close to sanctuary. We'd make it; somehow we'd make it . . .

More minutes dragged away. The river turned from deep brown to dull black, and all but a faint patina of daylight vanished from the heavens. I could see stars above us to the north—Polaris, the Ursa Major and Minor constellations—gaining brightness and definition like images developing on a strip of processed photographic film.

Ariana said "Dan!" and her fingers bit into my arm. I lowered my gaze from the sky.

A flickering of firelight had appeared at last on the far western riverbank: the village, the Senoi village.

"God," I said—and it was the closest thing to honest prayer I had thought or uttered in more than thirty years.

# 14

The village was laid out in a long, narrow clearing that fronted the riverbank, just beyond a hard northeast bend—maybe two dozen stilt-supported, palm frond-roofed *kajang* huts. Small, smoky fires burned at the entrances to nearly all of them. The natives saw us coming, and a knot of them, chattering excitedly, formed on the bank. When we were close enough for them to make us out clearly, I heard the words *orang puteh*—white people—and most of the women and young children broke away in fright. Those who stayed moved back, not speaking now, watching us warily, as Ariana and I poled the raft in against the bank.

My legs were cramped from kneeling in one position, and when I went over the side to beach the raft, they wouldn't immediately sustain my weight. I fell heavily to one buttock in the water and had to drag myself out, with one hand on the muddy bank and the other on the raft. Ariana crawled off, reaching for me, and I got hold of her and tried standing up again. This time I made it, right leg full of pins and needles. I pulled Ariana all the way up and steadied her against me with an arm around her waist.

The Senoi, naked except for loincloths made of bark, kept on watching us in stoic silence. They were under five feet tall and stubby-legged, with distended stomachs and tangled mats of black hair; wide eyes stared furtively from dark, brooding faces. I saw knives and blowguns, but they were not held menacingly.

Ariana said something to them in Malay dialect, her voice edged with fatigue. There was no response. She spoke again, in a sharper tone. One of them stepped forward then and answered her gutturally, with obvious reluctance. They began a slow and lengthy exchange.

When it was over she said to me, "I told them who I am, and of course they've heard of me. They're not as wild as some tribes; they'll help us."

"How?"

"By sending a runner to the estate in the morning, to the Malay kampong along the river. Then someone else will guide us to the perimeter. My father will come for us there."

"They won't send the runner tonight?"

"No. Even the Senoi would have trouble tracking the jungle in full darkness. We'll be given one of their huts—and food, I expect."

"All right," I said. "It doesn't matter much anyway; we're both dead on our feet."

The Senoi held a brief conference among themselves, and then four of the men moved off to a hut at the rear of the clearing. After a time they came back, and the one who had spoken earlier—maybe the chief, maybe not; some of the tribes are matriarchal—muttered half a dozen words and motioned for Ariana and me to follow him. We passed through the village, and I could sense dozens of eyes watching from the darkness. At the hut the spokesman pointed at it without speaking again, and immediately went away and left us alone.

There was a bamboo ladder of sorts leaning against the front, and we climbed that and entered the hut on hands and knees, because the enclosure was less than four feet in height. It contained nothing except four loosely woven rattan mats, half a dozen bananas, and two coconut shells partially filled with a dark glutinous substance; the four men had cleaned out everything belonging to the dwellers of the hut, as though they were afraid of contamination. There were no walls as such, although the roofing palm fronds covered most of the four sides more than halfway down. The faint glow of firelight penetrated and cut the heavy blackness enough so that we could see each other. Dank human effluvium seemed to waft up from the flooring like an invisible vapor.

I sank down crosslegged on one of the mats and picked up a coconut shell and looked more closely at the contents. The smell of it was foul. Ariana said, "It's probably a combination of cooked yams and *blachan*, a paste they make from half-rotted fish. I shouldn't eat any of it."

"I wasn't about to. The bananas look all right."

"As long as they're still unpeeled, yes."

We ate all six of them, three apiece, and draped the skins over the stuff in the coconut shells and pushed the shells over by the entrance. Outside, the village was hushed. There was a muffled scurrying in the fronds above us: lizards, probably, after the large ginger-colored Malaysian roaches. Sooner or later one or the other would drop down on the floor with us, but I didn't care at all about that; I couldn't hold my eyes open any longer.

I lay back supine with one of the mats over me and my hands under my head, breathing through my mouth, shivering in my wet, odorous clothing. Immediately, wordlessly, Ariana pressed her body against mine as she had last night, and again I held her.

Within seconds I was asleep.

In the night something woke me, and I jerked up into a sitting position. My head ached, my body ached, my eyes were gritty with mucus; even my bones seemed chilled to brittleness, though it wasn't nearly as cold as it had been the previous night. A tiger moaned loudly in the jungle nearby: a repetition, perhaps, of the sound that had dragged me out of sleep.

I rubbed at my eyes and saw that a pale shaft of moonlight had come in through the open entranceway, illuminating the hut in faint, ethereal light. I realized then that Ariana was no longer lying against me, and I moved my head quickly to look for her.

She lay on her back an arm's length away, the covering mat bunched around her hips from movement in sleep—and she was naked to the waist.

Rising and falling gently with her breathing, her breasts were starkly white against the tan above and below, except for three ugly leech bites on the soft skin between them and another a couple of inches above the left nipple. Her wet brassiere and jacket must have become unbearably clammy, maybe chafed on the sores, and despite the cool of the night she had removed them; both were lying to one side of her on the undermat.

For a long moment I couldn't take my eyes off her. In sleep and half-nude like that, she was the most alluring woman I had ever seen. She stirred as I watched her, moaned softly, and reached down without waking to pull the covering mat up over her; she drew her knees up, huddling. I moved to her, then, and lay on my back against her, but without touching her with my hands. I didn't look at her again.

And I didn't sleep much, either, the remainder of the night.

When I stirred out of a last restless doze, there was cold gray dawn in the hut. Ariana was dressed again, and like me she was moody and weak and in need of medical attention; pneumonia was a lingering threat. Neither of us had any desire to walk through that jungle again, even with a guide and even though the distance from the village to the Union Jack wasn't great. But when that walk was over, so would be the last of the ordeal—and the anticipation of that was enough to give us the stamina we'd need.

As we climbed down out of the *kajang* hut, I saw that by daylight the village had a depressing, utterly primitive look. At the rear of the clearing, rotting meat and fish sat on a pole arrangement, coated with flies and other insects; near it, a woman with one bare pendulous breast and a corrugated scar where the other should have been started out of the jungle, saw us, and retreated quickly. The huts and the areas around them seemed hushed and deserted: things wouldn't return to normal until after we were gone.

The spokesman for the tribe appeared abruptly from somewhere on our left, carrying two spiny durian fruits. He held a brief conversation with Ariana, then vanished again. The runner had already been sent to the Union Jack, she told me, and we would leave with the guide shortly.

The moment we finished eating—the durian is one of nature's little jokes: the custardlike pulp smells foul, but tastes ambrosially sweet—the spokesman returned with another, much younger Senoi. The young one, armed with a crude *parang* knife, wouldn't look at Ariana or me; there was no further dialogue.

He turned immediately and led us out of the village and into the jungle.

# 15

It took us the better part of an hour, on a network of native-worn trails, to reach the perimeter of the Quayles estate. The young Senoi set a rapid pace, and Ariana had to call sharply to him a couple of times to slow him down. He still wouldn't look at us. The jungle itself was less dense than that through which we had gone the previous day, and except for the inescapable and maddening onslaught of leeches and insects, it didn't bother me as much as I'd expected.

As soon as we came out of it, at the edge of a narrow sun-drenched downslope grown over with dry lalang grass, the young Senoi abandoned us with silent swiftness. Beyond the slope I could see one of the Union Jack's kaboons: tall, leafy, evenly spaced para rubber trees. A laterite road serpentined through it to our far left. There was as yet no sign of anyone else in the vicinity.

I took Ariana's hand and we made our way slowly down through the lalang grass, angling toward the road. The hot stark sun felt incredibly good, like a healing hand on my chilled body, but I had to squint against the glare; after the continual watery darkness of the jungle, the brightness cut like sharp needle points into my retinas.

We were on the kaboon, skirting the nearest of the rubber toward the road, when I heard the sound of an automobile engine—and a moment later a single vehicle traveling at a good clip came into view. It was a covered Land Rover, and there were two men visible through its windshield as it swung around toward us.

The driver saw us, and brought the machine to a squealing halt. He came out running. Ariana let go of my hand and hurried to meet him, and he embraced her and clung to her in almost fierce relief. He was in his early fifties, silver-haired, aristocratic-featured, tanned the color of old leather: Martin Quayles, of course. He looked almost exactly as I had pictured him, except that he was fairly short instead of tall and rangy.

I reached the two of them at the same time as the other man from the Land Rover. A middle-aged Malay, dressed in whites and wearing rimless glasses, he carried a black bag that stamped him, as it stamps men and women the world over, a doctor of medicine. He peered worriedly at Ariana and then at me; one glance at either of us was enough to concern any physician.

Quayles gave me a quick, penetrating look over Ariana's shoulder; then he returned his attention to her, stood her back away from him. He said in an anguished voice, "Good lord, Ariana, what's *happened* to you? I've been frantic, imagining all sorts of hideous things . . ."

She smiled wanly at him. "It's a rather long story, Father. Can't it wait until after we've got to the house?"

"Yes, of course," Quayles said, although you could see that he was aching for explanations. He turned to the Malay doctor. "Ahmad—have a look at her, man."

Ahmad took her arm gently and started her toward the Land Rover, asking professional questions in a soft voice. Quayles put his eyes on me again. "You're Daniel Connell."

"Yes."

He nodded, and then pivoted back toward the Rover. I followed him, went around to the passenger side. The doctor had helped Ariana into the rear seat, and he slid in beside her and opened his black bag. When I joined Quayles on the front seat, I saw that there was a World War II–vintage Webley revolver—for protection against snakes and straying jungle animals, probably—in a holster clipped to the dash.

He swung the car into a turn and built up speed. In the back Ahmad was sponging filth from cuts on Ariana's face and arms with cotton soaked in alcohol. She had her eyes closed, hands in her lap, breathing audibly. I turned my head to the front and stared out at the retreating surface of the road; the rapid motion funneled faint nausea into my throat. None of us spoke.

We crossed the Sungei Kerling on a wooden bridge, and two or three minutes later topped a rise and came down toward the estate buildings. The plantation house was set on a small hill to the left: a peaked white dwelling with wide verandas on the three visible sides and long windows open against the heat of the day. To its left was a lush garden, and well behind it was a tin hangar and the private airstrip Ariana had told me about. A line of coconut palms grew to the right; on the other side of them was a row of three small cottages, two huge tin-roofed structures that would be factory buildings, and another long, low construction. Farther along, on the river, Malay longhouses stretched to the edge of another rubber kaboon.

Quayles stopped the Land Rover directly in front of the plantation house. The front door opened as the four of us got out, and a middle-aged, sad-faced Malay appeared clutching his hands and looking concerned. "Have you got the rooms ready, Tan Chen?" Quayles called to him.

"Yes, *tuan*."

Ahmad and Quayles assisted Ariana up onto the veranda and inside the house; I went in after them. We were in a big, cool parlor filled with fine old anachronistic teak furniture, the sofa and chairs upholstered in batik. There was a ceremonial batik on one wall. Electric punkahs swirled on the high ceiling: rubber country air-conditioning.

Tan Chen led us through a bead curtain and down a long hallway on the right. At one of four closed doors, Quayles released Ariana's arm and pivoted back to me. Indicating the door, he said, "Guest room in there, Connell. You'll want to get out of those wet clothes and into a hot tub until Ahmad can attend to you."

He turned and followed the others down the hall to one of the other doors: Ariana's room. All of them except Tan Chen disappeared inside.

I pushed open the guest room door and went in. The bed was a double, covered with mosquito netting, and it looked damned inviting. To one side of it was a suitcase on a rack, and I recognized it as mine; Quayles, or the police, had retrieved it from the damaged jeep. I crossed to it, raised the lid. Everything was there, including the carry-all and the soiled clothing which had been bundled in K.L.—thrown into disarray, no doubt as a result of another search by Mutt and Jeff after they'd lost us in the jungle.

I closed the lid again, entered the adjacent private bath, and ran steaming water into a big, old-fashioned tub. When I stripped off my viscid clothing, a fresh chill washed across my shoulder blades. My skin was puffy, puckered, discolored, filthy. I got shaking into the tub. The water blackened instantly as I scrubbed away caked mud and grime, using the washcloth gingerly on the sorer areas. Then I opened the drain, let that water out, ran clean water and lay there soaking and waiting to get warm.

The chill dissipated again, finally, and the hot water helped to soothe some of the aching in my limbs. I stepped out, toweled dry, put on a thin cotton robe that was hanging on a hook opposite. In the bedroom again, I pulled the blankets back and then got into the bed under them.

After a time Ahmad and Quayles came in without knocking. Immediately, the doctor popped a thermometer into my mouth. I had a temperature, it turned out, but only a degree above normal. Ahmad produced a syringe and a vial of something from his bag and gave me a shot. Then he handed me two sets of pills—salt tablets to counteract desalination, and quinine as a preventive against malaria— and watched while I swallowed all of them with tap water from the bathroom. He uncovered me and opened the robe, probed at my body, used stinging iodine and a pinkish ointment on the cuts and scratches and parasite bites.

I said, "Miss Quayles—how is she?"

"She is weakened, and with fever, but her condition does not appear to be serious."

Silent until then, Quayles said to Ahmad, "You're quite sure they needn't go to the hospital at Kuala Ba?"

"There is nothing those at the hospital can do that I have not already done. The *mem*, and this man, need rest—much rest. They may have it here as well as at the hospital."

"Very well. But you're to stay here in the house the rest of the day, tonight if necessary. If there is even the slightest hint of complications, you're to tell me immediately."

A little primly, as though his professional instincts had been affronted, Ahmad said, "Of course." And there was a knock on the door. Quayles went over and opened it.

"Captain Piow is here, *tuan*," Tan Chen said.

"Show him down."

Quayles sent Ahmad back to Ariana's room, and Tan

Chen returned with a thick-bodied, scowling Malay who wore a khaki uniform and the local equivalent of a Sam Browne belt. Piow was chief officer of the police bureau at Kuala Ba, Quayles informed me. One of his patrol had found the jeep in the jungle stream, and he had been heading search operations for Ariana and me.

"Will you please tell us what happened, Connell?" Quayles asked then. "I'd rather not disturb my daughter at the moment."

I would have liked Ariana present for explanations, to lend support, but he was right in not wanting to disturb her. I said, "I'd better start from the beginning," and then I told them about Mutt and Jeff, and Kirby, and Maria Velasquez, and the mysterious Red Fire—skipping over my flight from the scene of Maria's murder and my anonymous telephone call to the K.L. police. They let me talk without interruption, but they didn't like any of it. Quayles's mouth was tight-lipped; Piow's eyes had narrowed into little slits of suspicion, and you could tell that he was wondering if I was really as innocent in the affair as I proclaimed.

Quayles said, "If these persons want you that badly, they're certain to have remained in the vicinity."

"I'm afraid so."

He looked at Piow. "You'll get your men on this immediately, Captain?"

"Yes," Piow said. Then, to me: "You will describe, please, these two men and the car they were driving."

I did that.

"You have no idea of their names?"

"No."

"Or their nationalities?"

"European, I think. I can't be any more specific than that."

"The name of the bank at which this man Kirby worked in Kuala Lumpur?"

"Barclays. His real name may be Kerwin, though. When the short one asked me about him on the boat, he used that name."

"He gave you no other information about himself?"

"Kirby? No."

"And the term Red Fire means nothing to you?"

"Not a thing."

Piow studied me with his narrowed, suspicious eyes. "Have you anything else to tell us, *Tuan* Connell?"

I knew I was going to have to explain about my past, because if I didn't he would find it out quickly through official channels, and it was much better if he—and Quayles —heard it direct from me. I said, "About Mutt and Jeff and Kirby, no. But there's something else you'd better know."

I gave it to them succinctly but without trying to soften the tawdrier aspects. I couldn't gauge Quayles's reaction; his face remained impassive, and his eyes revealed nothing. But Piow's reaction was easily readable, and predictable: skepticism, contempt, distrust. He had categorized me now—*penjahat*, criminal: once thus, always thus—and there was nothing I could say or do at this time, if at all, to convince him of the absolute truth of my reformation and my honesty.

He said in hard tones, "You deny that the men you call Mutt and Jeff are a part of your 'former life'?"

"I deny it because it's the truth. I've told you everything exactly as it is." My voice had begun to thicken, and it was an effort to keep my eyes open. The medication Ahmad had given me, and general fatigue and the warmth of the bed, had started to spread sleep like a heavy blanket across my thoughts. "There's an inspector of police in Singapore named Kok Chin Tiong who might vouch for me a little, and you can get in touch with him. Aside from that, I can't offer any additional proof except my word, whatever that's worth to you."

There was ten or fifteen seconds of silence. Then Quayles

said to Piow, "I expect he's told us all he can or will for the moment. He needs sleep, and we've the immediate problem of locating those two men—or rather, you have, Captain."

Piow was reluctant to let go of it, even for the time being. He would have liked to stand there and hammer questions at me, looking for inconsistencies, ready to pounce at the first opportunity. But this was Quayles's house, not the police station at Kuala Ba, and Quayles was obviously a respected and influential citizen in this area—not a man to be argued with. He nodded finally, gave me one last look, and turned for the door.

"You and I shall talk later, Connell," Quayles said to me, without inflection, and then followed Piow out into the hall. The door shut quietly after them.

I was asleep before the sound of their footsteps faded toward the front of the house.

# 16

There was somebody in the room.

I had been tossing restlessly, still asleep but nudging consciousness, and as though from a considerable distance I heard the sound of the door opening. Pale light fell across my eyes. My mind was so sensitive to danger, so hyper-aware of the threat of Mutt and Jeff, that I woke instantly and started off the bed, blinking against the light—an amber wedge of it coming through the open door from the hall, cutting through otherwise full darkness. I had my feet on the floor, tangled in the bedclothes, reeling on a list toward two dark shapes just inside the door and beyond the light, when the ceiling lamp snapped on and I saw who it was.

Quayles and Ahmad.

My knotted muscles relaxed, and I reversed myself and sank down onto the edge of the bed. I rubbed a hand across my face, scraping beard stubble. There was a faint throbbing in my head, and I felt somewhat weak, but it was the kind of weakness you have when you've broken a heavy fever. The bedsheets were damp and smelled sourly of sweat and of the pinkish skin ointment.

I said, "God, what time is it?"

"Quarter of ten," Quayles answered. He nodded to Ahmad, and the doctor came forward and handed me a cup that contained warm chicken broth. While I drank some of it, he laid a hand against my forehead and took my pulse. Then he wanted to know exactly how I felt, if I had pain anywhere.

I responded, and after I had I asked Quayles, "What's going on? You didn't wake me up just for another examination."

"No." Quayles looked at Ahmad, who dipped his head but looked faintly disapproving. "I wanted to find out if you were up to a drive into Kuala Ba."

"Now? What for?"

"I've just had a call from a subordinate of Captain Piow. They've caught one of the two men, apparently, and they want you to make a positive identification as soon as possible."

My spirits lifted considerably. "That's damned good to hear," I said feelingly. "Which one is it? Where did they get him?"

"I don't know which one; they got him on the outskirts of the village. We'll be given the particulars when we arrive. You do feel up to it tonight?"

"To get a look at even one of those two in custody, I'd crawl up off a deathbed."

I finished the last of the broth, put on my last clean bush jacket and a pair of trousers from my suitcase, and then went into the bathroom and had a look at myself in the mirror. Red eyes in an unpleasantly hued stranger's face—mottled purplish-yellow, thin scratches the color of flame, three days of gray-black beard stubble—stared back at me. But the swellings, at least, had receded there and on my arms and neck.

I came back into the bedroom, and Ahmad insisted I swallow more pills and put on a heavy coat which belonged to Quayles. Then Quayles and I went out of there and through the house to the rear, walking softly. Ariana was asleep, of course, and when Quayles said she was "resting easily," the relief in his voice was evident. I held my own relief inside me.

Attached to the back side of the house was a kind of portico, and the Land Rover was parked beneath it. The night was fairly warm, well-scented with the fragrances of tropical flowers and shrubs. I began to sweat inside the heavy coat, but better that than a chill and another flirtation with pneumonia.

When Quayles had driven us around to the front, onto the main access road, I saw two men armed with rifles patrolling the grounds. We passed the nearest of them, and Quayles said, "One of the first things I did this morning was to post guards here, along the roads, and in the rubber."

I nodded, watching the headlights sweep the road ahead of us.

Quayles said, "Captain Piow, you know, was of the opinion that you should be held in protective custody, either in the hospital or the police station, until both men are caught and your background could be checked more thoroughly."

"Because of the threat to you and your daughter?"

"Yes."

"You didn't agree with him, evidently."

"No. As long as even one of those men remains free, Ariana and I are in a certain amount of danger no matter where you are."

I didn't like the thought of it, but that was true enough.

The police couldn't keep me under wraps indefinitely, and all either Mutt or Jeff would have to do would be to wait until my release. I could get out of the area entirely, go back to Singapore or K.L.—but that wouldn't eliminate the threat to Quayles and Ariana. If Mutt or Jeff couldn't find me through any other means, there was the possibility of the kidnapping of Ariana or Quayles on the chance *they* would know where I had gone. And I just couldn't run out on people who were imperiled because of me—especially Ariana, with the way I felt about her now.

Quayles went on, "I spoke with Ariana when she awakened late this afternoon. She said you were quite honest with her in the jungle, and that you're a decent sort, and she believes you totally. I trust my daughter's judgments."

"Piow isn't nearly as generous or understanding, is he?"

"I'm afraid not."

"Did he contact Inspector Tiong in Singapore?"

"Yes. This man Tiong seems to back you up where your past is concerned, although not strongly enough to satisfy the captain. He's checking further, of course."

"There's nothing more for him to find."

"For your sake, Connell, I trust not."

We had crossed the bridge spanning the Sungei Kerling and were traveling now through one of the deeply shadowed kaboons. I said as we came on a fork and took the left artery, "This question may be a little premature, but when Mutt and Jeff are no longer a threat—what then?"

"Will I allow you to work for me, you mean."

"Yes."

"Tell me one thing: are there others like Mutt and Jeff, men from your past?"

"Who might pose another menace sometime? No. Absolutely not."

"Then as matters stand now, you may consider your position secure—provided, naturally, that you perform your duties properly and there are no additional problems. I don't believe in holding past mistakes against a man. What he is today is the only important consideration."

Ariana had called him a reasonable man, and so he was. I liked him, and if things worked out all right, I was going to like working for him. I said, "Thanks, Mr. Quayles. I hope you won't regret that decision."

"If I should, Connell, so shall you. I think we understand each other, don't we?"

"I think we do," I said.

When we came out of the rubber, I saw the entrance to the estate—an arched sign, similar to those you used to see in Roy Rogers and Gene Autry westerns, spanning the road, and sturdy wire fencing stretching away on both sides. A jeep was drawn up on the side of the road there, and two armed guards stood near it. Quayles made a gesture to them as we passed.

Some distance beyond the entrance, the road hooked to the left and entered the jungle. The thin moonlight was mostly obliterated then. I watched the dark shapes of trees and undergrowth rushing by outside the Land Rover: cold, alien, primeval. Nature is an awesome thing, I thought; you don't realize just how awesome until you've faced her on her own terms. When you have, and have been fortunate enough to win a small if bitter victory, you can only respect her, and fear her, the more.

A half mile or so from the estate, Quayles slowed as we came on a sharp left curve. We were just into it when the headlights picked up, suddenly, a huge horizontal form blocking the entire width of the road. Quayles jammed on the brakes, and in the glare I saw that it was a young oil palm tree. We jerked to a stop five or six yards away.

Quayles shifted into neutral but did not shut off the engine. He said, "Damned fallen trees—constant hazard out here. I'll see if it can be moved with the car."

He opened the door, stepped out. I didn't move. The jungle, closely edging the roadway on both sides, was thick and black; the heavy fronds of the oil palm seemed to absorb most of the illumination from the headlamps, like a giant blotter, so that the roadbed on the far side was mostly shadowed—but there was enough spill to the right to allow me a clear look at the bole. One edge of the bottom end was splintered; the rest appeared to be smoothly severed.

And all at once, with unequivocal intuition, I knew that the whole thing—the telephone call from "a subordinate of Captain Piow," the fallen palm—was a trap set by both Mutt and Jeff.

I shouted, "Quayles, get back inside!" and reached out at the same time to pluck the Webley revolver out of its dash holster with my left hand. I used my right to depress the door latch, hit the door with my shoulder, transferred the gun to my right hand as I came out standing, shielded by the door. Quayles had stopped two paces away on the other side of the Land Rover, and he was looking across at me as though I had gone mad.

"Get inside! It's a trap!" I yelled at him—and there was sudden movement in the jungle on my side, maybe thirty yards away. I saw a white face shine in the darkness, briefly, like a specter, and swung the Webley over there and squeezed the trigger. The gun bucked in my hand, rolling echoes of sound fled through the night, but I didn't think I'd hit whichever of them it was.

Quayles was moving then; he spun back around the driver's door, head down. There was a quick yellowish flare in the dark vegetation on that side, and a bullet spanged into the Rover's fender with a keening metallic sound. So they'd finally picked up guns somewhere. I put a shot in the direction of the muzzle flash, didn't hear or see anything over there, and ducked down inside the Rover again as Quayles slid under the wheel and slammed his door and fumbled for the gearshift.

The one on my side cut loose twice, missing us entirely both times. I swung my door shut, and Quayles got the transmission into reverse and let the clutch out. We bucked backward, weaving. He twisted his head around to look out through the rear window, left hand on the wheel and right on the stick. His face was hard and slash-lipped, eyes flashing. After fighting first the Japanese and then Communist guerrillas, he knew how to handle himself once he realized a crisis.

We skidded back into the curve. At the far perimeter of the headlight beams, I could see one of them running out onto the road from the right—Jeff—and then the short one appear on the other side. Quayles reversed us all the way through the curve, cutting off my view of them; cramped the wheel and braked. The Land Rover bounced to a halt just long enough for him to shift into first, then we snapped into a tight forward turn, scraped foliage on my side, straightened out. He hit second gear, and third, putting his foot down hard on the accelerator. The road behind us stayed dark; even if they had a car in the vicinity, and it figured that they had, they probably wouldn't give chase, with us so close to the estate and with the jump we'd gotten. They had put all their cards into the trap—and again, just barely, they'd lost the hand.

Belated reaction set over me, and I was conscious of a faint trembling in my hands, the weakness in my legs and shoulders. A thin sheen of sweat coated my face. I wiped the wetness away, put the Webley back into the dash holster, and bunched the coat tighter around me.

Quayles said with contained rage, "Close back there. Too bloody close."

"They must've gotten Piow's name in the village," I said. "And when they had the spot picked, they cut through the palm until it was ready to fall, and then one of them went back to call you. As soon as that one returned, they felled the tree and settled in ambush. Time element adds it up that way."

"Resourceful buggers."

"Yeah. You still think I ought to stay on at the Union Jack, Mr. Quayles?"

He didn't hesitate. "Certainly. It's a personal matter now; I don't take at all well to being shot at. And I expect your quick reactions just now may well have saved my life."

"You got us out of there in a hell of a fine hurry," I said. "That makes us even on that count."

He glanced at me briefly, put his eyes back on the road. We came back onto the Union Jack, then finally over the rise and down toward the plantation house: home free, at least for the time being. Quayles stopped the Land Rover by the front stairs, and when we were inside the house he made straight for the telephone. I stood by while he put a call through to the police bureau in Kuala Ba. Captain Piow wasn't there at this time of night, but Quayles spoke with someone else of authority and told what had happened in sharp, terse words.

When he'd rung off he said to me, "Men will be dispatched immediately, but I should doubt they'll find anything—not tonight, in any case. They'll come in person from now on if there is anything to report; I shan't be fooled the same way twice." He smacked his right fist into his left palm in nervous agitation. "The only thing I can do here is double the guard patrols. As long as we remain on the estate, we shouldn't have to worry."

I didn't feel nearly as confident of that as he seemed to, but I supposed he knew well enough about safety measures, having survived the guerrilla terrorism of the fifties. Still, Mutt and Jeff were worse than ordinary fanatics; ideology can't hold a candle to old-fashioned greed in the inspiration of resourcefulness, tenacity, and brutality.

Quayles said, "You look a bit staggery. I should think you had better get back to bed."

"Right. But you'll call me if you hear anything definite?"

"Of course." He paused. "My daughter shouldn't be told of what took place tonight, not yet. I don't want to worry her."

"Just as you say."

He went out and I went to the guest room, thinking grimly that unless we got a break somewhere along the line, the next move—like the last few moves—would belong again to Mutt and Jeff. . . .

# 17

When I came into the parlor late the following morning, Tan Chen was putting a vase of freshly cut flowers on one of the polished teak tables. There was no one else about.

"*Selamat pagi, tuan,*" he said gravely.

I returned the greeting.

"You are better today?"

"Much better. Is Miss Quayles up?"

"No, *tuan*. She is still asleep."

"Mr. Quayles?"

"He has gone out into the rubber."

"Do you know if there's been word from Captain Piow?"

"There has been word, yes—but not good word."

"The two men still haven't been found."

He nodded sadly. "You are hungry, *tuan?* Some tea and cakes?"

I hadn't had anything to eat except the chicken broth in the past twenty-four hours, and though I was hardly ravenous, I needed something solid on my stomach. I told him tea and cakes would be fine. He went away, and I walked to a pair of open glass doors that led to the west-side veranda and looked out over the lush garden, the coconut palms beyond, the rubber and then the jungle to the horizon. Heat shimmered wetly in a sky streaked with cirrostratus clouds.

Surprisingly, I had spent the night in a deep rather than restless sleep. I still felt somewhat enervated, but I was evidently on the road to full recovery; even the aching stiffness in my limbs seemed to have mostly abated. I'd taken a warm shower after rising, and then, from a tube Ahmad had left on the nightstand, applied a fresh coating of skin ointment to all the discolored areas on my face and body. My facial skin was far too tender to even consider shaving.

Tan Chen returned with a silver tea service and a tray of Malay cakes and set them on a carved teak sideboard. He poured tea into a china cup and went out again. The cakes were warm and sweet, made from rice and sugar, and the tea was strong; I felt better still once I had had some of each.

I opened the glass doors and went out onto the veranda and sat in the sun for a time, watching huge green and black birdwing butterflies fluttering lazily in the garden. When it got to be too hot, I stepped down into the garden and, slowly, walked around there for a time in the shade. Finally, bored with that, I came back onto the veranda and re-entered the parlor.

Ariana was there, sitting on the batik-covered sofa and sipping more of Tan Chen's hot, strong tea.

She wore a flowered silk Chinese robe with long sleeves, and she had brushed her hair until it shone glossily. Her face, like mine, was without swelling, and she had managed to conceal some of the skin discoloration with artfully applied makeup. She looked very tired, but her eyes were clear. And her overall appearance, encouragingly, said that she wouldn't be suffering any complications either.

I said, *"Tabé, mem."*

She glanced up. "Well," she said, "at least one of us is a bit more than ambulatory today. How do you feel?"

"Better than I should."

"You look a fright with those whiskers."

"I know. How do *you* feel?"

"Weak, but otherwise chipper."

"No fever or anything like that?"

"Not a bit. It seems we're a rather durable pair."

"As much lucky as durable."

"Mmm. Have you been up long?"

"About an hour."

"I take it there has been no report on Mutt and Jeff?"

"None worth mentioning," I said.

"Have you spoken with my father?"

"Last night, yeah. At some length."

"About your past, I expect."

"That, and some of my future."

"Which means, of course, he hasn't sacked you."

"He hasn't as long as there's no more trouble." I sat down on a chair across from her. "He said you'd stood up for me, and I appreciate that. But I can't help wondering exactly why, after what you've been through."

She gave me her faint smile. "You've been through the same as I—and more. A person reveals his intrinsic qualities most honestly in a crisis, don't you think?"

"Meaning you approve of whatever I might have revealed about my real self out there in the jungle."

"Meaning that, yes."

"What would that be, specifically?"

She would have answered my question, and the conversation might have gone on then to an even more personal level, if Quayles and Ahmad hadn't picked that moment to come in through the front door. And for one reason and another—mainly Ahmad's insistence that Ariana spend more time

119

resting in bed—we didn't see each other alone again the remainder of the afternoon.

Dinner that night was a mildly spiced Nasi Padang—the multicourse Malay equivalent of Indonesian curry. Conversation centered at first on Mutt and Jeff. Captain Piow had called again: still no word on their whereabouts. As a result of last night's attempted ambush, he had assigned a unit to patrol the main road and estate roads and had also replaced Quayles's guards on the house with men of his own. A check with Barclays Bank in K.L. had determined Kirby's real name to have been Kerwin, all right—Richard Kerwin—and the bank confirmed that they had, as he'd told me on the *Pangkor*, fired him two months ago for heavy gambling propensities. Barclays didn't know anything more about him. And the Singapore police had nothing on him, either, nor could they offer a make on Mutt and Jeff on the basis of descriptions alone.

Once we had exhausted that topic, Quayles began talking rubber, including a lot of statistics on the annual latex yield of the Union Jack and each of its primary kaboons. I asked sporadic questions, and Ariana did not say much at all. She seemed to be in something of a brooding mood.

At the end of the meal Quayles decided he would forgo coffee, saying that he had some ledger work to attend to. "We'll have a tour of the estate tomorrow, Connell," he said to me. "You can begin with your duties on Saturday or Sunday, if Ahmad allows it."

Then he kissed Ariana, said good night, and left us there in the dining room—finally alone again.

She said, "You'll have coffee, won't you, Dan?"

I nodded, and she summoned Tan Chen and told him we'd have it on the west veranda; the weather was mild enough, and we were well enough, so that the night air presented no threat of physical retrogression. We went out there and settled into rattan chairs near the railing. Chinese lanterns suspended from the eaves gave off thin orange light and attracted silver- and emerald-winged moths and a host of other flying insects, but hanging braids of citronella grass helped to keep away the mosquitoes. Around to the front, wind bells tinkled musically in the faintest of warm breezes.

Tan Chen brought out a silver coffee service that matched the tea service of the morning, poured two cups, and then disappeared again, all with silent deftness: the perfect houseman, virtually invisible. I lifted my cup and looked out at the pale gold half moon suspended like an immense, half-lidded eye above the black jungle. Ariana stirred sugar into her coffee and sat holding the cup without drinking, her eyes focused straight ahead.

It was two or three minutes before either of us spoke. Ariana said then, "You know, Dan, I love it out here: the primitive beauty, the solitude, the rubber, all the satisfactions of estate life. And yet, I'm quite bored with it, too, at times; I find it all impossibly dull and meaningless." She put the coffee down again, untouched; she didn't look at me. "I am twenty-six years old and I know precisely what I want from life and I am perfectly content. But then, there seem to be a great many things I'm missing altogether, you see, and I am not content at all. I . . . well, that all sounds terribly ambivalent, doesn't it?"

"A little," I said, and I had the feeling she'd wanted to say those things, and more, to someone for a long while; that she hadn't been able to say them to her father. And I had the feeling, too, of a rekindling of the intimacy between us which had been interrupted earlier by Quayles and Ahmad—a different and even stronger intimacy than the one we had shared three nights ago in that jungle glade.

She turned to me, and her eyes roamed my face in the pale

lantern light. "What do you think of me, Dan Connell?" she asked softly. "What sort of person did *I* reveal myself to be out there in the jungle?"

"I'm not sure I can answer that, Ariana," I said. "You're a lot of different persons, and I can't make up my mind which of them is the real you. From what you've just told me, you don't know which it is either."

She was silent for a moment. Then: "I was quite the bitch to you in K.L., wasn't I?"

"Yes."

"I knew it at the time, of course, but I did it anyway. I seem always to act that way when I've only just met someone, no matter who he or she might be. A defense mechanism, perhaps; I don't know. I've never made friends easily."

"Is having friends important to you?"

"Not especially, though there are times when I feel lonely and I wish I had a great many friends."

Without thinking I said, "What about lovers?"

The bluntness of the question didn't seem to bother her. "I've had lovers," she answered. "In London and in K.L. and in Singapore. None of them ever really mattered."

"What does matter, Ariana? I mean, really matter?"

"I simply don't know. Oh, there are superficial things, but nothing *moves* me. New and exciting things do for a while—I was excited when those men were chasing us in the jeep, you know, and excited when we first were certain we were lost—but then the exhilaration changes to something else: fright, anxiety, boredom. I'm afraid I shall go through my entire life being half-stimulated by certain things, then losing interest in them entirely, and I don't think I could bear that . . ."

She let her voice trail off; and then, abruptly, she stood. "I believe I'll have a walk. It's a lovely night for walking."

I started to rise. "I'll go with you . . ."

"No," she said. "No, Dan, not tonight."

She went down off the veranda and into the garden and was gone.

I sat there in the warm stillness. I thought I might have a vague understanding of why she had confided in me as she had, and maybe of why she had so suddenly terminated the conversation, but I couldn't be sure, and I told myself not to jump to any conclusions. Still, I kept thinking of the things she had said and what they could mean in relation to me; and of the night by the jungle fire, and the moment I had almost kissed her, and the feel of her body pressed against mine; and, like a kid, I thought of the way her naked breasts had looked in the moonlit *kajang* hut.

I had it bad, all right.

And when you've got it that way, sooner or later and no matter what the consequences, you have to force the issue; you have to make something happen, either way. You have to *know*.

# 18

Quayles and I left the plantation house at dawn, in the Land Rover, for his promised tour of the Union Jack. He wore riding breeches and a Port Dickson hat today, and in that outfit he looked every bit the *tuan besar* of a fairly large estate.

Rubber was the only topic of discussion, and had been since I'd met him for tea and toast in the dining room. Ariana had still been in bed. Ahmad wanted her to take it easy at least one more day, which was why she wasn't joining us on the tour.

Our first stop was the Malay longhouses along the Sungei Kerling, where Quayles made sure the native *mandors*, or foremen, had the workers up and on their way to their respective kaboons. Then we drove out into the rubber, and on both sides of the narrow laterite estate roads the lines were spreading out to their appointed tasks among the striped trunks and dew-heavy leaves: low tappers, high tappers with ladders, lalang diggers, disease-control teams, timber-clearing gangs. When Quayles brought us finally to the three small, contiguous kaboons I would be handling, the sun had climbed up off the eastern horizon and the cool morning air had begun to gather heat. The acreages were out on the northern perimeter of the estate, hard against the jungle, one of which looked to be in pretty good shape but the other two of which—unproductive for the past seven years—were heavily overgrown.

Quayles parked the Rover at the smallest and seediest of the three, and we got out. "As you can see, Connell," he said, "these kaboons need considerable work."

I nodded. "It figures to be quite a job, all right."

"I'll expect you to have them in shape within two months."

"I'll do my best, Mr. Quayles."

We walked through the thick shade of the rubber, avoiding the taller patches of lalang grass. The trees were in fruit, and now and then you could hear loud cracking sounds as pods burst in the warming sunlight and scattered their seeds; the smell of them was richly exotic. It was all just as I remembered it from my brief experience in Ipoh, and I liked the atmosphere as much as I had then. My job here on the Union Jack offered a great many things: hard satisfying work, a degree of challenge and responsibility, a certain communion with nature, a sense of peace.

And yet, there was the way I felt about Ariana. . . .

When we returned to the Land Rover, Quayles drove us through more of the rubber. He stopped periodically to check work in progress and to introduce me in turn to each of his two chief overseers: sun-weathered Britons named Chadwick and Rexford. Both were polite and sympathetic in a reserved way and seemed genuinely agreeable to my presence on the Union Jack, probably because I represented a certain lessening of their work loads. I would get along fine with each of them, I thought, as long as I was careful to pay due respect to their experience and seniority.

It was shortly past ten when we came back onto the grounds proper of the estate. Quayles parked between the two tin-roofed factory buildings, and we went inside one of them. Tappers had already begun to file in with buckets of milky latex—tapping is done almost solely during the morning hours, since the sweltering heat of midday and afternoon slows down the flow of sap from the trees—and Malay *mandors* were supervising weighing and testing activities. All of the equipment was clean and modern, including the row of aluminum vats at the upper end. The vats contained coagulating latex and were heated by gas fires that made the interior furnace room hot; sweat began to run on my face as we started a right-to-left circuit.

There were workbenches along both side walls, and narrow aisleways running parallel to them. The center of the concrete floor was cluttered with slabs of coagulated latex, stacks of tapper's cups, the testing apparatus and weighing scales, timber-clearing tools, twin backpack tanks of fungicide and insecticide, and a welter of other items. On the far wall was an extensive collection of *parang* and tapping knives, some of which may have still been in use, others retired antiques; one tapping tool that I recognized, with a thin hooked blade and a revolving disc attachment for regulating the depth of the cut, was called a Tisdall's and had been outmoded for at least fifty years.

Quayles kept up a running commentary, explaining procedures, answering the occasional questions I put to him. By the time we had come back to the entrance doors, I knew all I'd need to know about the processing of the latex for shipment to K.L.

He took me briefly into the second factory building, similar to the first, and then we went around to the long, low structure that ran perpendicular to and apart from the factories at their upper ends. This was a combination mess hall and plantation dispensary, staffed by native cooks and by Doctor Ahmad; it also housed a small mercantile store where workers could buy clothing and a variety of staple supplies, and where I bought a package of cigarettes. Like many rubber estates of its size, the Union Jack was something of a self-contained community, although not nearly so much a one as it would have been during the turbulent early fifties. At that time, smallholdings as well as large company estates had been under constant terrorist attack from the bands of jungle-based Communist guerrillas. Thousands of trees were slashed, buildings were set afire, planters and their families were brutally murdered. It had gotten so bad that whites and some Chinese in Malaya hadn't dared to venture forth during daylight much less nighttime hours without armed bodyguards and in anything but armored vehicles. Some of the larger plantations had even employed their own private militia forces. But through British and Malayan military campaigns, led by men like General Sir Gerald Templer, the bandit menace had been first controlled and then all but eliminated by 1960. Nowadays, except for isolated incidents mostly concentrated near the Thai border, the only real threat to individuals comes from tropical disease, and to the trees from occasional elephants that break through fencing and trample young saplings in the kaboons.

A hundred yards to the west were the three small cottages. Set side by side, fronted by little porches and separated by flowering hibiscus and jacaranda, these were the quarters occupied by the overseers. The one nearest the factory buildings would be mine, Quayles said. He took me inside, and it wasn't much—tiny kitchenette, stall bathroom, main room with a bunk-type bed covered by mosquito netting, an old wooden dresser, a rattan chair and table; but then again it was certainly no worse than the flat I had had in

Singapore's Chinatown, and would do me nicely enough. Quayles told me I could move in that afternoon, now that I was well enough to leave the main house.

We walked back to the Rover, and drove then onto a narrow road that paralleled his raised airstrip. The tin hangar at the far end gleamed in the hot, bright sun. I had been uncomfortably anticipating a tour of the hangar and his plane, but halfway along Quayles turned the car off toward the house. Apparently he respected my feelings about planes; he didn't even mention his own penchant for flying.

Ariana was in the parlor when we came in. She was dressed in khakis, hair well brushed, and she gave off the musky scent of mimosa perfume. The discoloration of her skin had begun to fade, as had mine—I had even managed a patchy shave—and her makeup concealed it more effectively than on the previous day. She was in good spirits, maybe even a little too buoyant. Her eyes would meet mine in that frank, steady gaze of hers, and then flick away. I would have given a lot to know what she was thinking.

Tan Chen served tiffin on the west veranda, and in the middle of it Captain Piow showed up. He scowled at me, disliking me openly with his narrowed eyes. You could tell he didn't care at all for the idea of my being allowed to sit at table with the Quayleses; if he'd had his way I would be eating my lunch in a jail cell. Stiffly, he declined an invitation to join us and reported a single new development in the hunt for Mutt and Jeff: the little blue Japanese car they'd been using had been found abandoned near a deserted tin dredge two kilometers from Kuala Ba. It was a rental vehicle, from an agency in K.L., and the man who'd rented it had given as identification an International Driver's License issued in Switzerland to someone named Pronzini; but a check of the number and name had proved it out to be a forgery. Fingerprints had been taken from the car—modern criminology extends even to remote areas like this one—and were being sent to Singapore and K.L., among other places, in an effort to get a positive identification on Mutt and Jeff.

Piow asked Quayles if they could talk in private—about me, I supposed—and the two of them went around to the front. I pushed my half-eaten lunch away and lit a cigarette and smoked broodingly. Ariana watched me without speaking.

After a while I said, "I guess it's time I moved myself out," and stood.

"Will you come for supper tonight?"

"I don't think I'd better. I'm a hired hand, not a guest, and I've already used up more than my share of special privileges."

She was silent for half a dozen seconds; then, in a voice void of inflection, she said, "Perhaps not."

"Meaning?"

She shook her head. "We'll talk again—soon."

"Soon," I said.

I went inside and down to the guest room and loaded up my bag. When I came back into the parlor, I saw through the glass doors that Ariana was no longer at the table—and when I got outside, there was no sign of either Piow or Quayles. I took the bag to my cottage, cutting through the grove of palms, and unpacked it again; then I visited the commissary and bought a carton of cigarettes. Coming back from there, I ran into the chief overseer named Rexford and briefly we discussed the kaboons that would be under my charge. He would meet me out at the number one late tomorrow morning, he said, to help me get started; he and Chadwick were going into K.L. for the night and wouldn't be back until then.

I spent the rest of the afternoon wandering around, looking things over again. Before returning to my quarters I had something to eat in the mess hall, swallowing it automatically and without enjoyment. My thoughts were full of Ariana, and of Mutt and Jeff, and between them they made me feel restless and edgy. I sat out on the cottage's tiny porch, smoking, watching the daylight fade into a brief sunset and then moonlit darkness. The flames of scattered fires flickered distantly at the Malay longhouses on the river. It was very quiet, except for the swelling hum of cicadas, and cool and peaceful.

A few minutes before nine, Ariana came.

She appeared out of the palms, walking slowly, and stepped up onto the porch. Her features were intense, and she wet her lips and looked at me in that steady way of hers. Neither of us smiled.

"All settled in?" she asked.

"Everything's *senang*," I said.

"I was out walking, and I thought I'd stop by."

The way she said that told me it wasn't exactly the truth. A kind of crackling magnetism seemed to be developing between us, and I knew then why she had come, I knew it was time, and with hunger beginning to pulse warmly inside me I stood up and moved to her and said softly, "I've been thinking about you all day, Ariana."

"Have you?"

"You know I have."

"Yes," she said.

"It's the same for you, isn't it?"

"Yes."

Her eyes were huge and dark; her mouth trembled slightly. The fragrance of her was like the surrounding fragrance of hibiscus and jacaranda: sweet, exotic, musky. And she said, "Dan . . ." and then came up hard against me—soft, soft mouth and sweet breath and warm tongue and straining body and my hands in her hair and down over her back and God, I wanted her! The kiss lasted a long time, and we were both breathing heavily when we broke it. I ran my lips along her jawbone and along her neck, and felt her shiver, and heard her make a muted sound deep in her throat. But then, not without reluctance, she drew back and put her arms between us, palms gentle on my chest.

"I'm not ready for anything more than this," she said. "Not tonight, not yet."

I touched her cheek. "All right."

"I want you very much, I've satisfied myself of that. But I'm afraid of another affair like all the others—I'm afraid of my feelings, or basic lack of them."

"Aren't you being a little hard on yourself?"

"I just don't want to be hard on you."

"I'm not naive, Ariana. I know all the potential pitfalls."

"And right now you don't care. But what of later?"

"Later is later. Life is full of unassurances."

"I still need a bit of time."

"Then take as much as you need; I won't press you."

She started to say something more, shook her head and kissed me again instead—just a small pressure of her lips. And turned and hurried away without looking back.

I watched her until she had vanished again into the palms. Then I let breath out in a long, blowing sigh and lit a cigarette and got myself calmed down. Just kissing her, holding her, had stirred me more than fifty sessions in bed with fifty different women.

Would she come again? I thought she would, I thought her desire was as strong as mine—too strong to be denied. And a simple affair, no guarantees, just two people getting to know each other and fulfilling their immediate needs together, *was* enough for me right now. Maybe we both needed something more one day, something lasting—maybe my feelings for her were deeply rooted, and vice versa—but there can be no future without a beginning, no building of a relationship without a foundation of closeness and mutual insight, no benefits without risks of some kind or another. You pays your dues and you takes your chances in all things.

I lay on the bunk-type bed and tried to sleep, and it was useless. Finally I got up and left the cottage and walked down by the river; walked out into one of the kaboons and was stopped by a guard who recognized me and suggested politely that wandering around in the darkness might get me shot by accident; walked back around the upper ends of the factory buildings. It was almost midnight by then, and I thought I had managed to make myself tired enough so that I could get to sleep.

I passed between the two buildings and started out around the one's lower end toward my quarters. I had my head up, looking toward the cottages—and the tall figure of a man was moving in low profile along the front of mine: a stealthy, mobile shadow faintly silvered by the moonlight.

I stopped automatically, hackles rising on the back of my neck, but I was in open ground and as clearly visible to him as he was to me. When he saw me he hesitated for an instant and then abruptly reversed direction, started to run with his right arm swinging up and clutching what was unmistakably a gun.

Jeff.

# 19

The coldness on my neck deepened, and a rush of venomous fury hammered at my temples. They'd made the one bold move I had feared all along—coming onto the estate after me; and despite Quayles's and Piow's intentions to the contrary, at least Jeff and probably Mutt too had clearly succeeded in getting past all guards and police patrols.

I reacted almost as quickly and instinctively as Jeff just had: spun back the way I had come, ducked around the corner of the near factory building. And other thoughts, even more chilling ones, began tumbling through my mind as I ran in close to the wall: *How did he know where to find me, which cottage was mine . . . he was coming from the direction of the plantation house . . . oh Jesus, they must have not only gotten past guards and patrols but taken Ariana and Quayles and forced them to tell where I was . . . is Mutt there in the house now . . . the bastards, the bastards, if they hurt Ariana I'll cut their goddamn hearts out . . .*

But I couldn't even consider going to the aid of Ariana and

Quayles until and unless I somehow managed to overcome the immediate threat of Jeff. I looked around desperately. There was no cover anywhere in the area between the two structures, nothing I could use as a weapon; the mess hall and dispensary building was more than a hundred yards distant and completely dark; the nearest guard was too far away to hear a cry for help. Trying to outrun him in my semi-weakened condition had to be an exercise in futility, and I damned well couldn't chance stopping and facing him in a head-to-head confrontation. He would want me alive, but I was pretty sure he'd fire anyway, risk the noise of a shot and aim for my legs, if he decided it was the only way to capture me.

I was nearly abreast of the factory entrance doors now— and suddenly I remembered the collection of tapping and *parang* knives I had seen during the tour earlier. If I could get inside, one of those *parangs* and the darkness would balance the odds. But Christ, wouldn't the damned doors be locked at night . . . ?

I looked back over my shoulder, and he was just rounding the corner forty yards behind me. That cemented the necessity for an instant decision; it was the factory or nothing. I veered to the doors, caught the latch on one, and threw my weight against the corrugated tin facing. The doors bowed in slightly but didn't part, and the latch wouldn't turn in my hand. Locked, all right. Frantically, I hit the one door with my shoulder, just above the lock, putting all my strength into the lunge. There was a short, sharp screech of snapping metal and the door halves split inward, vibrating. I lurched forward and down to one knee, but I was inside.

I came up staggering, regained my balance. Jeff was so close behind me that I could hear not only the sound of his running steps but the accelerated rasp of his breathing. I dodged around the door to the right, into the long narrow aisleway on this side. I went ten or fifteen steps like a blind man in the hot, heavy darkness, hands extended in front of me. Then my knee brushed against something, and one groping hand touched a hard metal surface: one of the big, thousand-pound weighing scales. I dropped into a crouch beside it, turning my body, looking back toward the entrance doors.

Faint light came through the opening from outside—and Jeff's silhouette appeared there, a single step inside and facing in my direction. Then he moved, and I heard the creaking of hinges as he started to swing the doors shut. The windows in both side walls, smoke-grimed to opacity, were little more than vague gray patches; when the light at the entrance disappeared, I couldn't see Jeff at all.

The solid wall of darkness and the maze of goods and paraphernalia covering the center floor made it impossible for me to cross directly to where the *parang* knives were located on the opposite wall. I'd have to follow the aisleway to the upper end and make my way around in front of the aluminum cooking vats. I backed away from the scale, moving crabwise, trying not to give my position away by banging into something.

I had gone no more than a few feet when a slender beam slashed an abrupt tear in the darkness.

Flashlight—he had a goddamn flashlight.

The whitish cone illuminated a section of the workbench on my left, probed toward me. I threw myself flat and crawled behind a row of the coagulated latex slabs, twisted my body until I was up on hands and knees. The light swung over the slabs, held there, slid away, came back. I could hear his footsteps, approaching cautiously; the angle of the beam altered as he neared the slabs.

The flashlight had tilted the odds back strongly in his favor, but in a small way it benefited me as well by providing enough diffused illumination so that I could see what lay around me. I propelled myself on elbows and knees along the row, around the far end of it just before he came abreast. Pieces of heavy machinery blocked passage on my right, but there was enough room between them and the latex slabs for me to slip past.

I got to the end of the machinery just as the flash swept over it from behind. To the right I could make out a small cleared space verged on the far side by testing apparatus; beyond that was the opposite aisleway. I scuttled to the equipment, started to squeeze through. My leg hit something, dislodged something else that clattered to the concrete. The beam darted over. I pulled myself into the aisle, then bellied at an angle across it and came up against the workbench. Sweat stung my eyes; I sleeved them clear, looking up at the wall. The light, moving restlessly over the testing equipment, was high enough to illumine the location of the knives, ten or twelve feet farther down.

When I had crawled to a point directly beneath the collection, I got my feet under me and held a breath. And then I levered up in a single rapid motion, clawed at the wall, ripped one of the machete-like *parangs* off its hooks. But in my haste I made small sounds doing it; the flash swept around, and this time found and pinned me in its thin white radiance.

I ducked down and ran in a low weaving crouch toward the lower end of the building. The beam wobbled—he was running too—and I tried to dodge away from it, cutting to cover behind one of the stacks of tapper's cups. Just as I reached it, there was the hollow reverberation of a shot, and I felt a sudden sharp burning across the back of my left calf. The area numbed instantly, and the leg went out from under me. Instinctively I held the *parang* out away from my body, and I didn't lose it and didn't cut or stab myself when I jarred sprawling into the concrete arrears of the stack, taking the impact on my left side.

I heaved up to elbows and knees again, shook my head

and shoved convulsively along the floor to an opening between two black metal drums. When I'd wedged through there, I could see the squared shape of a huge packing crate that had, I remembered, been turned into a scrap bin. I dragged myself behind the crate and got my back against it and sat there rigidly. Pulse throbbed in erratic cadence in my ears.

The light roamed out to the left, then lowered and steadied in small searching arcs. Jeff had come to a standstill back near the stack of tapper's cups—probably to listen for sounds that would help to reveal my exact position. I kept myself immobile, inhaling and exhaling the stagnant, sultry air in silent gasps.

A pall of silence settled throughout the building; and bitter, virulent frustration crowded down on me. Now what? The noise of the shot had apparently been muffled by the factory walls and hadn't carried far enough to alert anyone, so I couldn't expect any outside help. My calf was still numb—the bullet must have cut through muscle—and while I could still crawl all right, I knew I wouldn't be able to stand or walk until feeling returned. I had the *parang*, but without mobility it wasn't much good against Jeff's handgun.

Seconds crawled away, and the silence seemed to gain a magnitude that was almost deafening. But he would start coming again any second, and when he did I'd have to move too; if I stayed where I was, he would find me in short order. And yet, where could I go? I couldn't crawl rapidly and quietly enough to elude him, to fox him, to mount some sort of offensive or set some sort of trap . . .

Trap, I thought. Suppose I stayed right here, stretched out on my back and feigning unconsciousness? When he found me he'd have to come up close to where I lay, later if not sooner, and once he did that I could jump him with the *parang*. . . . Oh Christ, that was no good. He'd know a hoary old trick like that as well as I did, and there would be two obvious tipoffs: blood on my leg and nowhere else; and the *parang* visible in my hand or concealed along with my arm under my body, either way. And even if I *did* have the opportunity to make my move, there was the disadvantage of my numbed leg and unlikelihood of my being able to strike a crippling blow before he used his gun.

The frustration burned like gall in my throat, and I clutched the *parang* with such force that little lances of pain stabbed through my knuckles. I had a stark mental image of Ariana—and then of Maria Velasquez lying broken and dead in the K.L. shack. But I couldn't help Ariana until I helped myself. There had to be a way to take Jeff, there had to be *some* way. . . .

I heard him start to move again.

Reflexively, I pushed out from the crate and thrust myself to the right, away from the probing finger of the flash. With the light well behind me, I was unable to see much of what lay ahead until I was on top of whatever it was. Another weighing scale. A pile of picks and shovels and unwieldy double-edged axes. A leaning row of the twin backpack tanks of fungicide and insecticide.

And then a dead end: a six-foot-high stack of those black metal drums, arranged in a loose half square, that blocked passage completely on the three remaining sides.

I twisted my body around, and the light was exploring the area behind the scrap-bin crate. Feverishly, I scanned the immediate vicinity: no places of concealment, no close path of escape, nothing I could use to counteract the single major menace of Jeff's gun. The picks and axes were useless because of their size, the backpack tanks . . .

The backpack tanks.

Fungicide—insecticide!

I pushed forward, laid the *parang* down, and caught up the nearest of the units. The tanks—one of compressed air, one of the chemical—were two feet in length, lightweight, joined in the fashion of scuba gear. There were control valves on top of each, and extending from each were three-foot rubber hoses that came together in a short metal rod. At the end of the rod was a lever-operated spray nozzle.

Urgently, I opened both valves and then leaned forward from my knees like a Moslem praying and swung the unit over my back, pulled the fastening straps tight across my chest—making more small, unavoidable sounds in my haste. I picked up the *parang* in my left hand, took hold of the spray lever with my right. When I looked up, the light was a few feet to my left. The hazy white bulb of the flash itself was visible now, Jeff a vague shadowy outline behind it. He was maybe fifteen feet from me.

Closer, *closer*. Fifteen feet at least, just give me a minimum of fifteen feet.

The beam traced over the metal drums, dipped to the floor, flicked briefly to the right. He was still moving. One step, the light sliding back left, every muscle in my body screaming with tension, fingers tight around the spray lever; two steps, the light reaching for me; hesitation—keep coming! And a third step, less than fifteen feet—

And I straightened up on my knees, pushing the spray rod out in front of me, aiming a foot above the flash. In the same instant he must have seen me at the cone's perimeter; the light snapped over and struck my eyes, half-blinded me. But I held my arm steady and squeezed the lever all the way in, held it there, sending out a jet of the chemical solution instead of the fine mist you got with light depression.

The stream hit him before he could react, hit him exactly where I'd intended it to—full in the face. He screamed, and the gun went off wildly; the flash flipped out of his hand, tumbled in the air and spun bizarre patterns of light, hit something and then caromed off to the floor but didn't break. I lunged toward it, releasing the spray lever, transferring the *parang* to my right hand. Jeff continued to scream in shrill agony, reeling and crashing into things, creating a banging, clangorous counterpoint to his shrieks.

Then, just as I reached the flash, there was at once a tinny metallic clatter and a heavy, fleshy thud—and the screaming cut off in mid-octave, became a gurgle that became nothing at all. The quiet was absolute again. I swung the light around, located him almost immediately. He was lying in a motionless sprawl across one of the weighing scales, evidently unconscious; left hand clawed at his face, right hand at chest level and still clutching the gun.

The hot, stifling air was choked with the abrasive stench of insecticide. Coughing, trying to breathe, I kept the beam on him as I reached out to one of the drums and lifted myself onto my good right leg. The left calf had begun to tingle and throb, but I couldn't put any weight on it just yet.

I hobbled over to the scale, looked down at Jeff. His face was blistered and burned by the chemical, eyes swollen shut. Blood shone blackly on one temple. But he wasn't unconscious, as I'd first thought. He was dead.

In falling over the scale, he must have struck and then twisted his head some way; it was cocked at a lopsided, unnatural angle. He had died, fittingly and ironically, just as Maria Velasquez had died: of a broken neck.

# 20

My fear for Ariana's and Quayles's safety was principal now, and it maintained the taut level of need for urgent action. I stripped off the insecticide tanks, shoved the *parang* through my belt on the left side. The stinging pain had increased in my calf, replacing all the numbness, and I braced myself against the scale and leaned down to feel of the wound. Not much blood; it seemed superficial enough. I tested it for support, and though the pain intensified even more, it didn't buckle. I wouldn't be able to run, but at least I had a certain mobility again.

I bent a second time, pried the gun out of Jeff's stiffened fingers. It was an old six-shot Japanese military revolver. I broke the cylinder, and there were four cartridges left. Okay. If four weren't enough, no amount would be.

Using the flash to guide me, I limped through the clutter on the floor with as much speed as I could manage; came into the far aisle and went out through the doors. The area between the factories was still deserted, the mess hall dispensary still dark. The noise Jeff had made inside had seemed loud enough to rouse the entire estate, but again it must have been mostly contained by the thick wood-and-tin walls.

I shut off the flash and hurried in a kind of hobbled trot around the lower end, across in front of the cottages and then into the coconut palms. When I reached a point where I could see the plantation house, I pulled up against one thick, canted trunk and reconned the area. Light shone yellowly through the front shutters, which meant the parlor lamps were on; the rest of the house, as far as I could tell, was dark. Nothing stirred on the grounds, or on the access road, or anywhere within the range of my vision. Had Mutt and Jeff managed to kill or disable the guards stationed near the house, instead of just eluding them? I should have been able to see one or more of the sentries if they were still at their patrol posts. But I couldn't waste time checking on them; I had to find out what the situation was inside the house, I had to know if Ariana was all right.

I went laterally through the palms, until I was on a line with the rear of the house. Then I left their heavy shadow and looped around a pair of utility and gardening sheds, passed under the rear portico to where the Land Rover was parked. I paused there briefly to rest my throbbing leg, to listen. Cicadas sang in the garden, but the house seemed to harbor only silence and the night was void of any other discernible sound.

A row of pink hibiscus grew just beyond the portico, marking the garden boundary, and I found an opening in the shrubs and pushed my way through. Keeping to the cover afforded by the larger plants and bushes, I moved under a young flame tree and peered between the latticework of thickly angled branches at its base. Damn! Bamboo roll blinds had been lowered over the parlor windows and veranda doors; nothing showed through the tiny chinks except dull rays of lamplight.

I moistened stress-dried lips and wiped at my damp face. With my bad leg, I couldn't be certain of absolute silence if I tried climbing the veranda stairs and crossing for a look through one of those chinks—and that meant I didn't dare chance it. What to do now, then? Try the rear of the house? If the back door wasn't locked I could get inside, and the darkness would cover an approach to the parlor. There was still the threat of making a noise that would alert Mutt, but whereas the veranda was wood and given to sudden creakings, the inside floors were overlaid with smooth, solid marble and cushioning rugs. And I was familiar with the arrangement of rooms and passageways. And the quicker I got into the house, the better; there was nothing I could do for Ariana and Quayles out here.

I retraced my path through the garden and through the hibiscus, and stepped over to the rear stairs. Cautiously, experimenting with each runner before putting my full weight on it, I started up. The wood creaked anyway a couple of times, but not loudly enough to carry to the parlor. When I got up to the door I paused, but there still wasn't anything to hear from within. Be open, I thought, be open—and I reached out for the latch handle and slowly, carefully pushed down on it.

The door swung inward an inch or two under my hand.

I released a silent breath, edged a wider opening. The hinges made no sound. I slipped through, stood for a moment to let my eyes adjust to the deeper black. This was a narrow storage porch, with two doors opening off of it: one straight ahead to the kitchen, and one on my left to a short corridor that intersected with the longer side hallway off which the bedrooms were located. The side hall was the best approach, since Oriental rugs lined its full length and because of the bead curtain that partially obscured the parlor entranceway.

Once I could see well enough to risk moving, I started to the left. Bags of rice and meal were stacked along the inner wall, reduced to a single lumpy mass by the darkness, and I wasn't able to see what was hooked out from the far side until I stumbled against it with the point of my boot. I kept my balance, and the dull thump I made was barely audible even to my own ears—but the way the something had yielded put an iciness between my shoulder blades. I hunched over for a closer look.

It was a man's leg.

Awkwardly, I stepped over it and knelt down. Tan Chen. There was a huge, jagged gash in the side of his head, leaking blood, but he was still alive. Even so, he was in a bad way and it would be some time before he regained consciousness.

Rage boiled inside me, but when I straightened I kept a tight rein on it and forced myself to move deliberately. I went through the one door into the corridor, opened the other to the hallway, and put my head out to look up toward the bead curtain. Light spilled through and illumined the upper third of the hall. Parlor furniture and nothing else was visible through the hanging, colored-glass strands.

Edging out, I took two forward steps and then put my back against the near wall, the Japanese revolver held up close to my right ear. The house was deadly quiet. I slid silently along the wall, watching where I put my feet, gritting my teeth against the pain in my calf: past one doorway on this side, past the other, into the faint reach of light. When I had gotten to within a foot of the bead curtain, I leaned my upper body away from the wall in fractional movements. The front door came into my view then—and at least one occupant of the parlor.

Mutt was standing there with the door cracked, gun in one hand, peering out.

His odd-shaped eyes kept trying to blink, almost but not quite making it in that way they had. Otherwise, he appeared to be completely relaxed. If the tall one's continued absence was bothering him much, his face didn't show it.

I leaned out farther, an inch at a time, stretching my head until the cords in my neck were like taut iron bands. Chairs. The teak sideboard. The wall batik. One of the electric punkahs. An end table. The end of the batik-upholstered couch. . . .

. Ariana. And Quayles.

They were sitting stiffly on the far side of the couch, staring across at Mutt. She appeared to be unhurt and just as angry as afraid; her eyes burned with mute hatred. Quayles's face was gray and bruised and pimpled with sweat, mouth pulled into a thin grimace of pain. His left arm, held on one knee, was obviously broken: the elbow pointed grotesquely at the ceiling.

The small wash of relief I'd felt at first dissolved almost immediately into heightened tension and rage. They were alive, and Ariana at least hadn't been harmed, but the danger to them was still as great as ever. I put my gaze back on Mutt. Take him now, I thought, while he's alone there at the door and Ariana and Quayles are out of the line of fire. I brought the revolver up—but before I could step out and get myself in a position to shoot through the bead strands, Mutt pushed the door closed and pivoted away from it.

I stood frozen, watched him walk over toward the couch. He didn't glance in my direction. When he stopped near the end table, his back was three-quarters to me; but with Ariana and Quayles directly beyond him, I couldn't risk a shot. I took a calculated step forward, half-turned my body so that I had a better viewing angle. I kept the gun up and ready.

Quayles said, "Your bloody friend is a long time returning," to break the heavy silence. Despite the pain he was suffering, his voice was still strong and edged with contempt. "You don't suppose he's had trouble, do you?"

Mutt shrugged. "Look at your arm and remember your own resistance, and tell me then you doubt his abilities."

A flush crept through Quayles's gray pallor. "I'm not as young as Connell, or as strong. And I haven't gotten free of you on four separate occasions the past week."

"He will not escape again."

Ariana said, "For God's sake, we've told you and told you that Dan doesn't have this damned Red Fire you're after." There was fear in the words, as much for me, I thought, as for herself and her father.

"We know better. He has it, or has hidden it somewhere."

"He doesn't even know *what* it is!"

Mutt moved slightly to the left, into profile—still too close to them for me to act. "That much may be truth," he said. "Not many people would immediately recognize the card's purpose."

"Card?"

"A tiny plastic card. That surprises you, doesn't it?"

"What possible worth could a plastic card have?"

"None of itself. But it and the name Red Fire"—greed crawled into his voice—"are the keys to a quarter of a million American dollars."

"You're talking in bloody riddles," Quayles said.

The near corner of Mutt's mouth curved upward, exposing his gold tooth. "So? Then here is another: what nationality am I?"

Quayles and Ariana just stared at him.

"I am a Swiss," Mutt said.

He got no response to that either. They didn't have any idea what he was talking about. But standing there in the semidark hallway, trying to curb fervid impatience, I was pretty sure that I did.

146

During my smuggling days I'd had contact with a few men who had stashed large amounts of illegal cash in numbered Swiss bank accounts, and I knew a little of the procedures used by those banks. One procedure was the presentation to the depositor of a plastic card, similar to but much smaller than a credit card, which had nothing except the depositor's name on the front and a strip of magnetic tape on the reverse. The account number was encoded on the tape strip. The account was also assigned a special identification chosen by the depositor—mother's maiden name, a code name, whatever—so that when he wanted to make a withdrawal, he simply gave both the card and the verbal ID to a bank official. The card was inserted into a computer bank, the account number read off the magnetic strip; and if the number corresponded to the proper appellative, the bank automatically released on demand the funds in the account.

Red Fire, then, had to be the code name for an account in Switzerland containing a quarter of a million dollars. Mutt and Jeff apparently thought of the name and the card as a package, which was why Mutt had demanded "the Red Fire" when they'd braced me in front of Maria's shack in K.L.

The revelation brought up a host of new questions, but at this particular moment I didn't give a damn for further speculation or any more answers. All I wanted was for Mutt to get the hell away from Ariana and Quayles, so I could have a clear shot at him. But he kept on standing there in front of them, smiling faintly, pleased with himself and his little joke. He was a cool bastard—sociopathic and emotionless and as deadly as they came.

He said, "I think that is all I will tell you. It does not really matter if you know what the Red Fire is, but that is no reason to make it easy for you."

"Why doesn't it matter?" Quayles asked grimly.

"Once we have the card, there is nothing the police or

anyone else can do to prevent us from collecting our money."

"What do you intend doing with us when you leave here?"

Another shrug. "Nothing of consequence."

Ariana said, "Does that include Dan Connell too?"

"Of course. We want only the Red Fire."

That last was a lie—even if I had the account card and turned it over to them, they would have killed me; I'd caused them too much grief and frustration—and Ariana sensed this as well as I did. She slapped both hands against her knees in flaring anger. "You filthy shit!"

Quayles said her name in alarm, warningly; but Mutt wasn't disturbed. He puckered his mouth and made a kissing sound, and then laughed. Her eyes cut him into strips. He laughed again.

And finally—*finally,* the son of a bitch—he started away from them.

I stood statue-like, not breathing, muscles bunched all through my body. But his attention was on Ariana and Quayles as he moved sideways toward the front door. When he got to it he pulled it open a few inches again, put his back up against the wall. I eased the revolver forward until the muzzle parted two of the glass-bead strands, then held it rigid and lowered my head and peered along the iron top sights.

Mutt turned his head and looked outside.

Slow, slow, make the first one count—and I clenched my teeth and squeezed the trigger.

The revolver jumped, and there was a hollow concussion of sound. I heard Ariana cry out. A patch of blood like a bright red ink blot blossomed in the center of Mutt's chest; his head jerked around, and a look of pain and incredulity spread across his features. I shoved through the bead curtain in a shooter's crouch, aiming again—but I didn't need a second shot. The hand holding his gun came up part way, and then his eyes turned glassy and he folded at the middle and the gun clattered to the floor. He followed it an instant later.

I came all the way into the parlor and looked over at Ariana and Quayles. They were on their feet, white-faced with startlement and nascent relief. I limped to where Mutt lay by the door and bent to catch his shoulder and turn him. He was dead. I scooped up the gun and threw it and the Japanese revolver into a corner—and the tension went out of me like air out of a balloon, leaving me limp and weak-kneed.

I turned back to Quayles and Ariana, and they were coming toward me now. She didn't rush into my arms the way women are supposed to do in a situation like this; she didn't touch me at all; but her face and her eyes were full of feeling for me.

Quayles said in fervent tones, "I've never been happier to see a man in my life. I had nearly given up hope for you—for us."

I sank tiredly into one of the chairs. "Well, it's over now," I said. "The other one's dead too." I told them briefly what had happened with and to Jeff, how I'd come to the house and gotten in, how I'd waited in the hallway for the right time to make my move.

Ariana was looking at my leg with concern. "That wound must be ghastly," she said. "So much blood . . ."

"No, it's just a crease. But Tan Chen's still alive out on the storage porch and he needs attention damned quick. So do you, Mr. Quayles, from the looks of that arm."

He grimaced. "The tall one broke it like a bloody matchstick when I refused to tell them where you were. He threatened to do the same to Ariana. I had no choice then."

She said, "I'll go for Doctor Ahmad."

"Yes, and I'll ring up the police."

I fumbled in the breast pocket of my jacket for a cigarette.

None of us did or completed any of those things, because I'd been wrong a moment before—as wrong as a man can be. It *wasn't* over. Not by any means, it wasn't.

The chair I was sitting in was angled toward the front window, and I didn't see the kitchen door swing open. I heard it, but Ariana had stepped over that way and I thought it was her going out. But then there was the startled, sharply audible intake of her breath, and I saw Quayles's mouth drop open and his eyes pop wide like an actor pantomiming shocked surprise. I swiveled my head, and then came up convulsively to my feet and gaped in disbelief.

There was a man with bright, wild eyes standing in the kitchen doorway.

A man holding in his left hand, right forefinger hooked through the pullring, one of the deadliest of all small arms: a fragmentation grenade.

A man who couldn't be but clearly was Richard Kerwin, also known as Kirby.

# 21

In a macabre sense it was like looking at a reanimated corpse—what was left of a human being come back from a murky grave in the Strait of Malacca three hundred miles away. His clothes—not the same suit he had worn on the *Pangkor*, but baggy tan trousers and a white shirt—were wrinkled and dirt-streaked and tattered. His skin was blotched: fish-belly white and parboiled red. His cheeks were concave hollows under jutting cheekbones and the eyes appeared sunken in bone-ridged sockets, creating the illusion of his flesh having begun to decompose from his skull.

Only the eyes themselves were not in any way zombielike. What they *were* was the most chilling thing about him: the eyes of someone gone over the edge into madness.

He said in a thin, shrill voice, "I shouldn't move, not a step. I shan't like to blow us all to bits, but I shall, you know, I shall if you force me. Better that than the gallows. Better that than a ruddy slant-eyed hangman."

Crazy, all right. Whatever had happened to him since

Mutt and Jeff had pitched him off the *Pangkor*, however he had miraculously managed to cheat death in the icy, shark-infested Strait, must have been responsible. And that fact, coupled with the fragmentation grenade, made him even more dangerous than the other two. He could be bluffing in his threat to blow us up—he'd struck me as being cowardly as well as unstable on board the steamer—but I didn't dare gamble on finding out. His forefinger was tight through the grenade's pullring, and in his mental state he could jerk the pin in reflex as easily as on purpose. Most grenades like that were timed to explode three seconds after you released the lever handle contoured down from the top; even if I could get it away from him, the odds against my being able to get rid of it in time were prohibitive.

I glanced at Ariana, and her face was blanched but betrayed no overt emotion. On the other side of me Quayles looked bewildered and tense. The muscles and nerves in my own body were stretched wire-taut again. An apex of pressure, a full release, another apex—the human psyche couldn't stand that kind of strain indefinitely. Kirby—I kept thinking of him as Kirby—was bitter proof of that.

Quayles was the first of us to find his voice. "Who *are* you?" he demanded. "What are you doing here?"

Kirby made a giggling sound, like the chittering of a bat. "Ask Connell. He knows, he'll tell you."

Quayles shifted his eyes to me. I said flatly, "Kirby. Or Kerwin. The one who started this whole thing."

"But . . . you told us he was *dead*."

"I thought he was."

Kirby chittered again. "They couldn't kill me, tried but they couldn't do it. Treacherous buggers, promised they wouldn't harm me if I told them what I'd done with the Red Fire. Had to tell them, Connell, they saw me coming out of your cabin afterwards. And they had knives. Knives. Hate the beastly things, they terrify me. Guns too, but knives worst of all."

*Coming out of my cabin afterwards,* I thought.

And suddenly, in a rush of perception, some of the pieces started to fit together.

Kirby's visit with the arrack that night on the *Pangkor* . . . his being alone in the head for a minute or two while he washed his face and picked up the glasses . . . my carry-all case lying open on the sink. He must have known Mutt and Jeff were on board even before I mentioned it to him, and realized he was trapped, and decided in a panic to buy time by getting rid of the account card. What better person to lay it off on than me, the only one on the steamer he'd had any contact with? And what better place than one of the articles in the carry-all?

But why hadn't Mutt and Jeff found it when they searched the contents at Maria Velasquez's shack, later at the jeep after they'd chased Ariana and me into the jungle?

". . . pitched me overboard instead when that girl came out and saw us," Kirby was saying. He seemed eager to talk, as though words and explanation had been too long contained inside him; as though the sound of his own voice reassured him, the way it had on the *Pangkor.* "Major error on their part, didn't know I was an expert swimmer, oh very expert. Water was bitter cold, things moving in it, sharks, dark things—but I wouldn't die, I wouldn't die. Saw the lights of a boat, small boat, fishing boat. Thought I should never make it, but wouldn't die. Came close enough to call out and the captain saw me, picked me up. Bribed him with my last few quid not to turn me over to the patrol craft that came out . . ."

I thought: Maria Velasquez.

Sure, there it was. She'd admittedly sold one item from the carry-all, along with my new pair of jungle boots, for ready

153

cash in Malacca Town—the gold cigarette lighter. The plastic card would have been just small enough to fit inside a lighter of that size, wedged down into the cotton in the fuel section. That *had* to be it. Kirby had hidden the card in the lighter, Maria had stolen the lighter along with my other stuff and then sold it to an unidentified man on the street, Maria was dead and that meant there was no way either Kirby or I or anyone else could know who the buyer was. God, the irony! I had had the Red Fire all along, and yet I had been right in my claim that I'd never had it at all. And Mutt and Jeff had cold-bloodedly murdered the one person who could conceivably have led them to it.

"... took me a long while to get here from Malacca. Had to steal money. Stole this grenade too, from a house in Seremban. Needed a weapon. Guns there too but don't know how to shoot, and they terrify me. Finally arrived in Kuala Ba this forenoon. Had no idea if you were here, Connell, might have been dead or might not have the card any longer, but had to find out, had to know. Came out in a hired car. Guards at the entrance wouldn't let me in, wouldn't answer any questions. Thought I was a tramp. A tramp! Returned to the village and came upon a truck loaded with supplies for delivery here. Hid away in it. Clever, yes, very clever . . ."

How had he known where in Malaysia to come looking for me? Then I had that answer too. The letter from Quayles: it had been in my carry-all that night, and it had been written on Union Jack stationery. Christ, I might even have suspected him of reading it at the time, might have prevented everything else that followed, if I'd realized then—as I realized now—that he'd been calling me Conners up until his stay in the head but that after coming out again he had addressed me by my right name.

"... afraid to go looking about in the daylight, so concealed myself in the trees and watched and waited. Couldn't decide what to do with the guards patrolling round.

Then *they* came, Zimmerman and Ries. Killed at least one of the guards. Gave me a bad fright, seeing them, but I knew you were here then, knew the card was here too. Watched them, watched the house. Then later you came. Saw you skulking in the garden, then go round to the rear. Went up onto the veranda and watched through the blinds, saw you—"

Abruptly, he stopped talking; blinked a couple of times as if discovering just how long he had been going on. He looked from me to Ariana and Quayles. They knew how perilously unbalanced he was, and they were as motionless as I. The room seemed filled with static electricity.

"Someone may come," Kirby said. "No one in the area now but someone may come. Mustn't dawdle any longer." He was talking to himself, not us; his right index finger caressed the grenade's pinring. Then he focused on me again with those feverish eyes. "Your little toilet case, Connell—where is it?"

I hesitated. He wouldn't believe me, any more than Mutt and Jeff would have believed me, if I told him the truth: that the account card was almost certainly lost for good. The only thing I could do was build a lie, buy us all some time. His mental state made him deadly, but it also made him prone to mistakes in action and judgment; with enough time, with luck and a prayer, I might be able to find a way to disarm him.

I said, "You hid the card inside my gold lighter, didn't you?"

He blinked. "You found it?"

"Yeah, I found it."

"Where is it?"

"I don't have it anymore."

"Don't have it? What did you do with it?"

"I gave it to a friend."

"What friend? What friend?"

"A man named Piow," I said. Both Ariana and Quayles were looking at me, and I used Piow's name to tell them I was lying to Kirby and hadn't all along been lying to them.

"You're lying to me," Kirby said.

I started slightly. But he hadn't been reading my mind; his voice was petulant, almost imploring. I said, "No I'm not. You can search my belongings if you want. You won't find the lighter and you won't find the card."

"Where is this Piow person? Hereabouts?"

"No. In Malacca."

"Malacca!"

"That's where I got off the boat," I said. "Those other two were after me, and I did the same thing you did: put the card onto someone else to protect myself."

His face screwed up like a kid preparing a tantrum—and then, just as abruptly, it smoothed again. "No problem, certainly not. The airstrip, the hangar: you've a private airplane here. We'll *fly* to Malacca."

A blob of coldness crawled along my back. Oh Jesus, I thought. I should have said the card was in K.L., but I'd wanted it as far away from the Union Jack as possible. I hadn't even thought of Quayles's plane.

"Tonight," Kirby said. "Straightaway."

"Kirby, listen . . ."

But he didn't listen. He said to Quayles, "You're the owner here, the plane is yours. Must be able to fly it, mustn't you?"

"Have a look at this bloody arm of mine," Quayles said. "Do you suppose I can fly a plane with an arm like this?"

Kirby wet his lips, blinking again; then the eyes sought out Ariana. "Can *you* pilot the plane?"

"No," she answered stiffly.

"Shouldn't like it if you're lying to me."

"I know nothing about operating an aircraft."

He believed her—and his gaze returned to me. It had been

coming to this all along, as I'd known it would from the moment he had mentioned flying off the Union Jack. He stared at me for five or six heartbeats, and then: "You *can* operate an aircraft, can't you, Connell? Yes, of course you can. See it in your face."

Frustration and apprehension were strong inside me; I dug my fingernails into my palms to keep myself in tight check. "I don't fly," I said.

"Oh yes," he said. "Oh yes."

"Listen, you don't need the plane. You can drive—"

"Too dangerous, too slow. Flying is the only way. Have to get that card quickly, have to find enough money for airfare to Switzerland. Quarter of a million American dollars, heard Zimmerman say that while I was on the veranda. Knew it had to be a large sum, but not that large. Hundred thousand pounds, British sterling. Going to buy a place in London, going to be wealthy as a lord, won't let anyone stop me now."

"You can see the blood on my leg," I said, "you saw me limping outside. I couldn't work rudder or brake pedals . . ."

"Weren't limping that badly, standing all right now."

"The leg's liable to stiffen up—"

His face darkened with abrupt rage. "Shut up! I shan't stand for any more arguments!" He held the grenade up in both hands, finger almost white against the pullring.

There was a tightness in my chest, and I seemed to have difficulty breathing. I knew there was no way out of doing what he wanted, not now, not with the state he was in—but after what had happened on Penang, the way Pete Falco had died, I wasn't sure if I could even get a ship off the ground again. I was afraid of panic at the controls, of another crash, of a kind of latent, guilt-based death wish.

I said a little desperately, "Then just the two of us, Kirby. Alone. Leave them here, tie them up . . ."

"No. Oh no. *All* of us. Have to make certain I'm safe, mustn't take any sort of risk. All of us, I say."

I hesitated. With just Kirby and me in the plane, it wouldn't have mattered so much if I couldn't get it airborne, if we crashed; but with Ariana and Quayles along, I'd *have* to take it up and keep it up. Twenty years a flyer, wartime missions, peacetime late-night smuggling runs into hostile territory, thousands of takeoffs and landings and solo flights across half the globe and in all kinds of weather—but could I put a light plane into a clear night sky and fly it maybe three hundred miles?

Ariana had turned to me, and in a measured voice she said, "Do as he says, Dan." There was a kind of pleading command in the words, but in her eyes there was something else: trust, a belief in me that stated *I know what you're going through, but you'll do what has to be done because you have to, because all our lives depend on it.*

"Better listen to her," Kirby said. "Better do it."

I shut my eyes, snapped them open again. "All right," I said. "All right, goddamn you, I'll fly us to Malacca."

# 22

Quayles's plane was a six-passenger Lockheed utility transport maybe twelve years old and probably built in Italy, powered by a standard 260-hp supercharged Continental piston engine. Durable and operationally simplistic, it was the kind of light aircraft pilots who have flown F-86 Sabre jets and battered DC-3s would jokingly tell you they could jockey "half-blind and mostly crippled."

Just looking at it in the glare of the hangar's high-intensity lights, I felt my hands begin to shake and sweat pop out all over my body.

Kirby had ordered Quayles to give him all the money he had in the house, and then we had come directly to the hangar. There hadn't been anyone else abroad in the area. The night was shrouded in silence, and the sky overhead was a burnished black and studded coldly with pearl-button stars.

The sky overhead, the black night sky . . .

Behind me Kirby said, "Go along, go along, someone may come round to investigate the lights."

I moved forward to the near wing tip on legs which seemed hollow and rubbery. Kirby trailed Ariana and Quayles to one side of me, then raised the grenade and made an impatient pushing gesture with it—telling me to climb up.

I said automatically, "Preflight check."

"What?"

"I don't know the plane, I need to check it over."

"Is that necessary? Is it?"

I had my hands in my jacket pockets, so he couldn't see how much they were trembling. "I'm a pilot and you're not, Kirby," I said. I forced my voice to remain flat and rigidly controlled. "If you want to get out of here and back down again at Malacca, you'd best let me familiarize myself with the mechanics of it first."

"What Connell says is true," Quayles said. "Flying a plane isn't like driving an auto; you can't just hop into a strange craft and be off."

Kirby glanced nervously through the wide-open hangar doors, looked at me again. His eyes were even more furtive than they had been inside the house, his manner more agitated. "Quickly, then. Quickly, quickly."

With the three of them following I walked around the plane checking tires and brakes, landing gear alignment and gear strut, wings, ailerons, rudder, propeller, fusilage, fuel tanks. I opened the cowling on the pilot's side of the engine compartment and examined the ignition lead wires, magnetos, carburetor, oil tank. Moisture rolled down my cheeks and got into my eyes, and I had to keep rubbing it away with the back of one hand. In my mouth there was a taste like that of vomit.

I drained a pint of fuel through my hand onto the concrete floor, checking for water and dirt. It was clean. I wiped my hands and then closed and secured the cowling. The plane—as I had expected all along it would be—was well cared for and in good flying shape.

I said, "Okay," and went up onto the wing and through the door on that side. Ariana and Quayles came in after me, then Kirby. I tried to give Ariana a reassuring smile, but my mouth wouldn't seem to work, as if the muscles controlling it had ossified. I turned abruptly to secure the door; took a breath and went forward into the cockpit.

When I looked at the instrument panel, at the stick, a convulsive reaction started up in my stomach. The odor of my sweat was tangible in the close confines, raw and sour: the stench of fear. I put out one hand to steady myself against the back of the pilot's seat, and through the eye of my mind I could see the interior of the last cockpit I had been in, the one in my old DC-3 as Pete Falco and I flew low above the Penang jungle that night three years ago. . . .

*Pete turns to look at me; his face is pinched in the flickering light from the instruments. "How much farther?" he asks, and in his voice there is a touch of fright.*

*Stage fright, I think, and I smile. "It won't be long now, kid. Listen, relax, will you?"*

*"I don't know, Dan. I'm not cut out for this kind of thing."*

*I laugh a little to myself. It's his first time, and like my first time he is sitting there with a dry throat, hands that shake just slightly, stomach churning, asshole twitching. I laugh again, silently. He'll be all right. Once we get down he'll be just fine . . .*

Kirby said shrilly, "Why are you standing there? Sit down, sit down, start the ruddy engine."

He was sweating too, now. A tic had gotten up under his left eye, and it gave him the ludicrous appearance of winking. The fingers holding the grenade and its curved side lever clenched and unclenched; the finger looped through the pinring was taut against the metal—and I was sure I could see more of the pin than before, that he had already and unknowingly pulled it a fraction or two out of the body.

161

Three seconds, I thought. Three seconds, because there was no way I could take the grenade away from him after the pin was jerked free without the lever releasing. Three seconds: not enough time to throw it anywhere even if I could get my hands on it because there was nowhere *to* throw it. Three seconds, and a single fiery explosion that none of us would really hear. Three seconds, and shrapnel slicing into flesh, ripping flesh apart, ripping Ariana apart . . .

I shook my head sharply, stepped around the seat back. Kirby motioned Ariana and Quayles into the passenger seats directly behind me, Quayles at the window. Then he sat in the aisle seat to starboard, managed in awkward movements to buckle his seatbelt without letting go of either the grenade or the pullring.

I sat down and put on my own belt. The wound in my calf throbbed, but the pain was muted and I could move the leg and foot all right; I wouldn't have any trouble with the rudder and brake pedals. I gave my attention to the instrument panel. Flying is like swimming or operating a car: you never forget how to do it once you've learned. Automatic motions. Position check of gauges and toggles and controls. Taxi and running lights on. Fullest gas tank on. Magneto switch to L. Starter engaged. The engine caught immediately, and my eyes settled on the oil pressure gauge. It came up to normal.

I released the brakes, opened the throttle, gripped the stick tightly in my damp hands, and taxied slowly out of the hangar.

*Below us, dead ahead in the blackness of the jungle, I see the orange-yellow flames of signal fires. But there are only two of them, one on either side. I can only make out a small section of the strip; the rest is shrouded. Where have they built the two? At the head? In the middle? Where?*

*Pete leans forward on the seat, staring through the windshield. "I thought they were supposed to fire the length of the runway."*

*"Take it easy, kid."*

*"I don't like it."*

*"Cinch your belt. We're on our way . . ."*

There was still no one visible near the hangar or on the strip, no movement or lights anywhere in the darkness surrounding the estate buildings. The plane handled well, rolling smoothly on the graded asphalt surface. When I got it to the warm-up spot by the runway, I turned it into the wind for a final cockpit check. Engine running evenly at 1000 rpm, ailerons moving freely, elevator trim tab neutral, stick free through backward and forward range, rudder control okay, instruments okay, magnetos okay, static rpm at full throttle, idle rpm steady at closed throttle, primer secured—

*Kirby shouted, "Connell!"*

*Pete shouts, "Dan!"*

*I've put on the landing lights and I can see the strip clearly for the first time. It is short, much too short, and honeycombed with small holes and jagged cracks.*

*"Dan, pull out!"*

*"Shut up!"*

*"You can't land on that! This crate won't stand up!"*

*"Shut up, shut up!"*

*It is my decision, and I know what I have to do . . .*

"Take off, damn you. Take off!"

Kirby was leaning forward in his seat, face the color of paste and as wet as mine. And for the first time I realized that his heightened nervousness, his anxiety, was due to something more than a mad desire for escape from the Union Jack and recovery of the Red Fire.

He was afraid of *flying*.

God, I thought; God, what if I can't hold her steady down the runway? What if I have trouble getting us airborne? As tensed up as he is, any sudden jarring, any sign of adversity might damned well cause that one lethal reflex.

"Kirby, listen to me," I said urgently. "Ease up on the

163

pullring of that grenade. If we hit a bump, you could accidentally jerk the pin—"

"Don't tell me what to do. Know what I'm about. Piloting is your job. Mind it!"

I held off, but only for a second or two. The danger was just as great if I *didn't* take off and take off now. I had to put the Lockheed in the air cleanly, that was all. Put it up and keep it up in that velvet black night sky.

*"Pull out, Dan, pull out!"*

*"No! Can't you shut up!"*

*"You'll kill us both!"*

*"I can make it, hold on!"*

I *can* make it, I thought grimly. I can and I will, hold on.

I taxied into position on the strip, set the directional gyro and turned the carburetor heat off. Then I sleeved my forehead dry, and tried to ignore the painful shriveling sensation in my groin, and then released the clutch and opened full throttle. The plane began to run effortlessly. I found I had a death-grip on the stick and forced myself to relax it. I wanted to take another look at Kirby, but I didn't dare; I kept my eyes straight ahead, staring out through a blur of fresh sweat at the strip rushing by beneath our lights.

*The strip rushes up.* . . .

No, goddamn it, no! And I dredged up all the strength of will I had in me, drove the image of that night on Penang back into its shallow grave, blanked my mind and let instinct take over completely. We built up rapid speed, and once I sensed we had enough I eased back pressure on the stick. The nose lifted, the wheels left the asphalt—and we were airborne without even a shimmy.

I let out a shuddering breath, heard Quayles do the same behind me. Then I leveled the plane to gain airspeed, climbed to a thousand feet and went into a medium left bank, swinging out over the rubber to the west. At 2000 feet I moved the stick forward to the neutral position, set and locked the throttle, and trimmed the plane on a level, temporary course south by southwest.

I was soaked in sweat, but the rapid rate of my heartbeat had begun to decelerate and my hands were steady on the stick. My mind was clearing as well, and yet I had a vague feeling of disorientation, the way you do when you've just come out of a vivid nightmare. The events of the past few minutes seemed suddenly and strangely blurred, as if they had happened days ago instead.

It had been bad—but having done it and having survived it, I thought I could fly all right now, this one time, this one night. Unless the situation went beyond my personal influence and aeronautics became meaningless. Unless, accidentally, Kirby blew us all up with that frigging grenade.

I looked around at him. He had relaxed his grip on it, and his right forefinger was loose through the pullring now; he was staring at me with a kind of quivering relief, tongue exposed between his lips. But his eyes were still furtive, still alight with a paraphobia of flying.

"Well, Connell," he said, and chittered nervously. "Splendid. Quite nice, yes. Had me worried for a time, I daresay."

"Yeah." I blew out more air, and looked then at Ariana and Quayles. "It's okay," I said in a thick voice.

They knew what I meant, and Quayles nodded and Ariana let me see a wan facsimile of her faint smile. Both of them were shaky, but visibly that was all. A lot of women would have gone to pieces by this time, and a lot of men too; they were made of some tough fiber.

"Where are the charts?" I asked Quayles.

"In a plastic envelope on your side panel."

"Have you got fixed coordinates for Malacca?"

"No. I've never flown there."

"I'll work them out, then."

I glanced at Kirby again, then swung around and reached down and got the charts out. In doing that I couldn't help looking out through the side window. The jungle down below was a charcoal mass, stretching away to the horizon, and the sky was vast and empty except for a few stratocumulus clouds like puffs of dirty gray cotton to the east. The wild black yonder. Eagle-high and soaring. A hollowness developed under my breastbone, lingered until I pulled my eyes back to the instrument panel. Easy, I told myself. Easy now.

I opened the charts on my lap and put on the navigation light. Ariana and Quayles and Kirby were silent behind me; the only sound was the steady, pulsing drone of the engine. There was a large airport just east of Malacca, I saw by the charts, and two smaller ones a few kilometers north on the coast: one at Terendak and one near Sungei Udang. If the police were alerted before we arrived, it wouldn't make any difference where we landed; if they weren't alerted, one of the smaller fields was the best choice because you could come into one of them without a filed flight plan and arouse less suspicion than at a bigger field. A chance still existed of our being challenged—and if anyone got close enough to see that grenade, or even Quayles's broken arm and my wounded leg, there was no telling what might happen. But I couldn't worry about that now. We'd have to cross that bridge if and when we came to it.

Terendak, then, I decided arbitrarily. I fixed the longitude and latitude coordinates, folded the charts, and started to replace them in the panel envelope.

The plane began suddenly to shudder and wobble.

I snapped my head around, the muscles in my belly pulling taut. Kirby was leaning forward again with his eyes shining blackly. "What is it? What's wrong?"

I started to tell him it was nothing to be concerned about, that we'd hit a small pocket of rough air; but I was looking at his hands then, and I held the words stillborn in my throat.

In his fear he had temporarily forgotten about the

grenade; his right index finger was no longer pushed through the metal pullring.

I felt a small surge of hope. This was the first opening, the first chance for a move against him—and maybe the last; you could die waiting for more than one. But he was just out of reach of a backward lunge, and I sensed that I didn't have time to unsnap my belt and get to him before he could recover. If it had been a gun he was holding I might have tried it, but not with a grenade. He'd have to be totally distracted, terrified—so terrified that there would be almost no chance of him remembering the grenade—before I could gamble on jumping him. . . .

The plane continued to jounce, and Kirby said, "Quit your bloody stalling, Connell! What *is* it?"

Stalling, I thought. Stall.

And I had an idea, a maneuver that might just work.

There was no way of knowing exactly how he would react, and I still wasn't sure of my own reactions or of how the Lockheed would handle under stress conditions. But anything I did or didn't do from now on was a risk. If I went through the maneuver slowly, one phase at a time, checking on him all the way, I could abort the action at any time until the last second.

I knew I was going to try it.

I said quickly, "I don't know, I don't know what it is," and pulled my head around to Quayles, trying to tell him mutely to follow my lead, to trust me and not give the truth away. He'd been about to speak, but the intensity of my stare got through to him. He closed his mouth and took Ariana's hand with his good one.

"Do something, *do* something!" Kirby yelled.

Facing the controls again, I reached out and applied a little carburetor heat. We were coming out of the rough air and I did that just in time to cause the engine to stutter slightly and the plane to retain its vibration. "Engine's missing," I said and put apprehension into my voice.

"Missing? What do you mean, missing?"

"It's starving for fuel." I hoped that Quayles would understand what I was up to, find a way to convey it to Ariana so that when the time came both of them would be prepared.

I took the Lockheed up in a graduated climb, until the altimeter read 4,500 feet. The engine continued to stutter. When I glanced at Kirby again he was still leaning forward, still badly frightened—and his finger remained outside the pinring. It was still go, then. One more phase before the point of no return.

I dried my wet hands on my pants legs, and then I put back pressure on the stick to bring the plane's nose up sharply; applied more carburetor heat and cut the power to idle. It was outfitted with a stall warning device, and the horn began to blare loudly as we lost airspeed. Kirby made a bleating sound and I swiveled my head and saw him straining wildly at his belt. His left hand clutched the grenade in his lap, but his right was fisted up near his face.

The final phase was go.

"We've stalled!" I shouted. "Oh Christ, we're going out of control!" And at the same time I gave the engine a burst of power and applied full left rudder.

Immediately, the Lockheed nosed down and began to spin.

Kirby bleated again, hysterically. I maintained the spin with full up elevator and full left rudder, guts roped into knots; then lowered the elevator tab and let up on the rudder pedal, looked back and around. He had been flung hard forward and to the left against his seatbelt, and his eyes were glazed with blind, sick terror; his left arm was held petrified just off his left leg, the grenade angled toward the flooring, forgotten. There was less than a foot separating us now.

In one continuous motion I swung my feet off the rudder

pedals, braced them, and lunged up at Kirby. I caught the grenade and his hand in a sweeping upward motion, jerked the thing free. He didn't give any resistance; there was drool coming out of the corners of his mouth. I shoved the grenade into my right hand, bunched the fingers of the left and jabbed him karate-fashion full between the eyes. His head snapped back and his eyes rolled up and he went limp with blood starting to come out of his nose.

I pulled my body around again, wrapped my left hand and the last three fingers of my right around the stick—not releasing the grenade—and brought my right foot over and down on that rudder pedal. The plane had half-recovered from the spin by itself, the way a light aircraft will do as soon as you lower the elevator and let up on the rudder. I applied full right rudder, reduced back pressure on the stick, and the autorotation ceased completely. When I eased the plane to level flight, and raised the nose to the horizon, the altimeter read 2000 feet. I'd pulled it off with maybe five hundred feet to spare.

I trimmed the tab again, felt myself sagging with sudden and complete muscle laxity. Kirby was lying far over to the left, one hand dragging in the center aisle and the blood still coming out of his nose; I could hear him breathing in strangulated gasps. There was movement behind me, the click of seatbelts, and I saw Ariana and Quayles both rise. For the second time in less than two hours, their faces were animated with a kind of tremulous deliverance.

"My God," Ariana said reverently. "My *God*."

And that was all, just then, any of us was capable of saying.

# 23

The estate buildings were swarming with men and vehicles, the grounds ablaze with floodlamps and headlamps and interior lights, when I put the Lockheed into a descent for landing twenty minutes later.

"Looks like the police have arrived," I said wearily.

Wry-voiced, Quayles said, "Reinforcements after the battle has been fought and won."

"Yeah."

He had gotten a sheet of foam rubber insulating material out of a storage locker aft, and I had wrapped the grenade in that and secured the bundle with friction tape. Then he'd put it inside a tool kit, and the tool kit back into the storage locker. He sat guard over Kirby with a heavy wrench held in his good hand, but Kirby had shown no signs of regaining consciousness.

I'd told him and Ariana as much of the Red Fire story as I had been able to figure out. And Quayles had said that he'd known almost immediately that I was going to put the plane

170

into a spin—and why, having seen just as I had that Kirby's finger was no longer looped through the grenade's pinring; he had managed to whisper enough of it to Ariana to prepare her. Neither of them confided whether or not they'd harbored any doubts that I could both complete the spin and disarm Kirby, and I hadn't asked them. Ariana had been mostly silent, but once she'd leaned forward to touch my arm and her eyes on that occasion told me all I needed to know about what was going on in her mind.

When I landed the plane, cleanly and surely, I did not think about the night on Penang at all. But even though I had proven to myself that I could operate an aircraft again if necessary, I knew that in the future—barring another emergency—I wouldn't pilot this or any other plane. I *could* fly, yes, but whatever it is inside a man that makes him *want* or *need* to fly was still and forever dead inside me.

The police, led by Captain Piow, converged on the Lockheed as I taxied it to a stop in front of the hangar. There were questions and answers. Kirby, still unconscious, was taken away. We learned that the authorities had been summoned by Tan Chen, who had roused finally and managed to drag himself to the telephone. He had already been transported to the hospital at Kuala Ba, with a serious but not fatal concussion.

Hot coffee and stiff drinks in the mess hall dispensary. Quayles's broken arm set by Doctor Ahmad. The wound in my calf cleansed and bandaged. Bodies removed by ambulance: Mutt and Jeff, and two of the Malay police guards with their throats cut. Two men from the rubber work force assigned by Quayles to scour the plantation house parlor and remove—at least to the naked eye—all signs of the night's violence. Piow much less cool toward me, not accepting me exactly but willing to tolerate me now. More questions and explanations, and official statements.

It was almost dawn before any of us was able to fall exhausted into bed.

And it was ten hours after that, late Saturday afternoon, before we learned the rest of the Red Fire story.

I was up again, still tired but functioning, working on a cigarette, when Quayles sent word that Piow had returned from Kuala Ba. I walked from my cottage to the house—slowly, favoring my sore leg. Quayles looked pale but otherwise steady, Ariana looked somber and introspective, and Piow looked haggard. We had tea on the west veranda.

Kirby had been rational enough during interrogation, Piow said, to enable him to put most of the early pieces together in logical sequence. Additional details had come from the Singapore police and, through them, the offices of Interpol. It went this way:

As Kirby had told me on the *Pangkor*, he'd gone to Singapore looking for work after being fired from Barclays. He hadn't had any luck, and he was down to his last few dollars when he read an advertisement in the Personals column of the *Straits-Times*. The ad called for a man with banking experience for a discreet private negotiation. Kirby answered it, and met an American named Raifield at his hotel. Also present at that meeting were Mutt and Jeff—real names Zimmerman and Ries—both of whom were Swiss.

After a good deal of wary discussion, Raifield finally confided that he needed someone who knew banking procedure to help him withdraw a certain sum of money from a certain Swiss bank. Neither Raifield nor the other two could return to Switzerland personally, for reasons on which they wouldn't elaborate, and the complex Swiss banking law made it impossible to telephone or cable for withdrawal. The depositor *could* telephone and identify himself by giving the account code name and then authorize a representative to act in his behalf; but that representative had to appear in person—identify *himself* by delivering the code name as well—so as to sign the necessary papers. The account card could then be given to the bank's branch in Singapore, and if everything was in order on both sides, the funds could be transferred to and withdrawn from that branch.

Kirby wasn't told how much money was involved in the transaction, but he got the idea from Raifield that it was considerable. Raifield, on the other hand, offered Kirby a round-trip plane ticket to Geneva and two thousand dollars. Kirby said he would think it over, and made an appointment to see Raifield again later that same day. The more he considered, the more he decided that two thousand dollars was a paltry sum compared to what was apparently in the account itself. He had long dreamed of riches, and maybe his mind had already started to go on him; in any case, he determined to doublecross Raifield if he could.

He returned to Raifield's hotel at the appointed time, and found the American alone. He said he would accept the offer. Raifield had anticipated this, eager for his money, and had already made arrangements with his Swiss bank. He also had plane tickets for a flight out of Singapore that night. He gave the tickets to Kirby, then told him the identification name: Red Fire. And realizing that this was his one chance, acting on impulse, Kirby managed to catch Raifield off guard and struck him down with a heavy table lamp; crushed his skull.

Half-panicked, Kirby searched Raifield's body and found the account card in his wallet. There were a few dollars in the wallet as well, and Kirby also pocketed those. Then he ran out of the hotel room—and straight into the arms of Mutt and Jeff. There was a struggle and Kirby managed to escape, but not before he had lost the airline tickets. He was still in a panic, and his only thought was to get out of Singapore as rapidly as possible. But he didn't have enough money for airfare, and he was afraid to try the bus or train terminals. So he went instead to Collyer Quay, looking for inexpensive boat passage to some place, any place, where he could work for or steal enough money to buy a one-way ticket to Geneva. The boat he picked, which was just preparing for departure, was of course the *S.S. Pangkor.*

Mutt and Jeff had managed to trace him to the docks— probably through the trishaw driver who had taken him there from the hotel—and had then found out by asking at the steamship ticket office that he'd taken the *Pangkor.* They had driven or hopped a train to Batu Pahat, the steamer's first stop, and boarded it there. Kirby had seen them almost instantly, and had then gotten the idea to hide the account card in my belongings.

I had lived the rest of it.

The background on Raifield, and on Mutt and Jeff, was simple enough. Based in Geneva, Raifield had been an international fence of stolen paintings and other artwork, and a sometime financier of the actual robberies themselves; Mutt and Jeff were his detail men. All three of them had fled Switzerland—and Europe—because Interpol had tied them to the theft of a private collection in Munich and put out a blanket arrest warrant. Most of Raifield's money was in the Swiss bank, and knowing this, Swiss police had been watching the bank for any sign of him or his henchmen. But Swiss banking law prohibits police access to the records of all such institutions unless the police have proof that the money is stolen or resultant from criminal activity, which proof they did not have conclusively in this instance; so the authorities had no way of knowing the account number and therefore no way of watching the account itself. Raifield's scheme for getting his money out of Switzerland would have worked if Fate—my old nemesis, guised this time as a shabby little down-on-his-luck Englishman—hadn't stepped in to begin a chain reaction of terror, hardship and death.

When Piow had gone, Quayles and Ariana and I continued to sit on the veranda. She had her chair positioned close to mine, so that her arm touched my arm, and the mimosa fragrance of her hair was thick and sensual in my nostrils. We didn't talk much, watching it grow dark again. Now and then Quayles would look at us, without expression, and I was sure that he sensed the feeling between Ariana and me; I wondered what his own thoughts were.

Finally he stood. "Bloody arm's bothering me. I believe I'll retire again."

He kissed Ariana on the cheek, and then said to me, "You'll begin work tomorrow, Connell. I'll come round at dawn, and I expect to see you on the job by then."

"I will be, Mr. Quayles."

"Two months with those kaboons. Not a day longer."

"I'll try for six weeks," I said.

"Fine."

When he was gone inside the house, Ariana said softly, "He knew we wanted to be alone. There isn't much that escapes him."

"Do you think he approves of a relationship between us?"

"Even if he didn't, he wouldn't presume to intervene. He has always allowed me to make my own decisions, right or wrong."

"*Have* you made a decision yet—right or wrong?"

"I think you know I have."

"I hoped you had."

"No guarantees. I still don't know what I really want."

"If you want *me* for now, that's enough."

Our eyes held for a long moment. Then she stood and extended one hand to me. "Come, Dan," she whispered.

I got to my feet and took her hand, and we walked around to the front. Looking out over the estate from there, smelling the unique scent of the rubber, the perfume of frangipani and hibiscus and jacaranda—the perfume of Ariana—I thought solemnly of this ancient and exotic country in which we lived. Malaya—considered by some to be the legendary land of Ophir, from which the ships of King Solomon sailed home with spices, silks, gold and jewels. And maybe they were right. Maybe underneath a layer of surface tarnish from the touch of "civilized" man, Malaya was in spirit a legendary land where you could, if you lived long enough and were lucky enough, find peace and whatever other treasures you might seek.

I held Ariana's hand more tightly, and we went down off the veranda and let the night enfold us as we started through the palms to my cottage.

# FINE MYSTERY AND SUSPENSE
# TITLES FROM CARROLL & GRAF

| | |
|---|---|
| ☐ Allingham, Margery/MR. CAMPION'S FARTHING | $3.95 |
| ☐ Allingham, Margery/MR. CAMPION'S QUARRY | $3.95 |
| ☐ Allingham, Margery/NO LOVE LOST | $3.95 |
| ☐ Allingham, Margery/THE WHITE COTTAGE MYSTERY | $3.50 |
| ☐ Ambler, Eric/BACKGROUND TO DANGER | $3.95 |
| ☐ Ambler, Eric/CAUSE FOR ALARM | $3.95 |
| ☐ Ambler, Eric/A COFFIN FOR DIMITRIOS | $3.95 |
| ☐ Ambler, Eric/EPITAPH FOR A SPY | $3.95 |
| ☐ Ambler, Eric/STATE OF SIEGE | $3.95 |
| ☐ Ambler, Eric/JOURNEY INTO FEAR | $3.95 |
| ☐ Ball, John/THE KIWI TARGET | $3.95 |
| ☐ Bentley, E.C./TRENT'S OWN CASE | $3.95 |
| ☐ Blake, Nicholas/A TANGLED WEB | $3.50 |
| ☐ Brand, Christianna/DEATH IN HIGH HEELS | $3.95 |
| ☐ Brand, Christianna/GREEN FOR DANGER | $3.95 |
| ☐ Brand, Christianna/FOG OF DOUBT | $3.50 |
| ☐ Brand, Christianna/TOUR DE FORCE | $3.95 |
| ☐ Brown, Fredric/THE LENIENT BEAST | $3.50 |
| ☐ Brown, Fredric/MURDER CAN BE FUN | $3.95 |
| ☐ Brown, Fredric/THE SCREAMING MIMI | $3.50 |
| ☐ Browne, Howard/THIN AIR | $3.50 |
| ☐ Buchan, John/JOHN MACNAB | $3.95 |
| ☐ Buchan, John/WITCH WOOD | $3.95 |
| ☐ Burnett, W.R./LITTLE CAESAR | $3.50 |
| ☐ Butler, Gerald/KISS THE BLOOD OFF MY HANDS | $3.95 |
| ☐ Carr, John Dickson/CAPTAIN CUT-THROAT | $3.95 |
| ☐ Carr, John Dickson/DARK OF THE MOON | $3.50 |
| ☐ Carr, John Dickson/THE DEMONIACS | $3.95 |
| ☐ Carr, John Dickson/FIRE, BURN! | $3.50 |
| ☐ Carr, John Dickson/THE GHOSTS' HIGH NOON | $3.95 |

- [ ] Carr, John Dickson/NINE WRONG ANSWERS — $3.50
- [ ] Carr, John Dickson/PAPA LA-BAS — $3.95
- [ ] Carr, John Dickson/THE WITCH OF THE LOW TIDE — $3.95
- [ ] Chesterton, G. K./THE MAN WHO KNEW TOO MUCH — $3.95
- [ ] Chesterton, G. K./THE MAN WHO WAS THURSDAY — $3.50
- [ ] Coles, Manning/ALL THAT GLITTERS — $3.95
- [ ] Coles, Manning/THE FIFTH MAN — $2.95
- [ ] Coles, Manning/THE MAN IN THE GREEN HAT — $3.50
- [ ] Coles, Manning/NO ENTRY — $3.50
- [ ] Collins, Michael/WALK A BLACK WIND — $3.95
- [ ] Crofts, Freeman Wills/THE CASK — $3.95
- [ ] Crofts, Freeman Wills/INSPECTOR FRENCH'S GREATEST CASE — $3.50
- [ ] Dewey, Thomas B./THE MEAN STREETS — $3.50
- [ ] Dickson, Carter/THE CURSE OF THE BRONZE LAMP — $3.50
- [ ] Disch, Thomas M & Sladek, John/BLACK ALICE — $3.95
- [ ] Eberhart, Mignon/MESSAGE FROM HONG KONG — $3.50
- [ ] Eastlake, William/CASTLE KEEP — $3.50
- [ ] Farrell, Henry/WHAT EVER HAPPENED TO BABY JANE? — $3.95
- [ ] Fennelly, Tony/THE CLOSET HANGING — $3.50
- [ ] Freeling, Nicolas/LOVE IN AMSTERDAM — $3.95
- [ ] Freeman, R. Austin/THE EYE OF OSIRIS — $3.95
- [ ] Freeman, R. Austin/MYSTERY OF ANGELINA FROOD — $3.95
- [ ] Freeman, R. Austin/THE RED THUMB MARK — $3.50
- [ ] Gardner, Erle Stanley/DEAD MEN'S LETTERS — $4.50
- [ ] Gilbert, Michael/ANYTHING FOR A QUIET LIFE — $3.95
- [ ] Gilbert, Michael/THE DOORS OPEN — $3.95
- [ ] Gilbert, Michael/THE 92nd TIGER — $3.95
- [ ] Gilbert, Michael/OVERDRIVE — $3.95

☐ Waugh, Hillary/A DEATH IN A TOWN     $3.95
☐ Waugh, Hillary/LAST SEEN WEARING     $3.95
☐ Waugh, Hillary/SLEEP LONG, MY LOVE     $3.95
☐ Westlake, Donald E./THE MERCENARIES     $3.95
☐ Willeford, Charles/THE WOMAN CHASER     $3.95
☐ Wilson, Colin/A CRIMINAL HISTORY OF
   MANKIND     $13.95

# FINE WORKS OF FICTION AND NON-FICTION AVAILABLE FROM CARROLL & GRAF

| | | |
|---|---|---|
| ☐ O'Hara, John/A RAGE TO LIVE | | $4.95 |
| ☐ O'Hara, John/TEN NORTH FREDERICK | | $4.50 |
| ☐ Proffitt, Nicholas/GARDENS OF STONE | | $4.50 |
| ☐ Purdy, James/CABOT WRIGHT BEGINS | | $4.50 |
| ☐ Rechy, John/BODIES AND SOULS | | $4.50 |
| ☐ Reilly, Sidney/BRITAIN'S MASTER SPY | | $3.95 |
| ☐ Scott, Paul/THE LOVE PAVILION | | $4.50 |
| ☐ Taylor, Peter/IN THE MIRO DISTRICT | | $3.95 |
| ☐ Thirkell, Angela/AUGUST FOLLY | | $4.95 |
| ☐ Thirkell, Angela/CHEERFULNESS BREAKS IN | | $4.95 |
| ☐ Thirkell, Angela/HIGH RISING | | $4.95 |
| ☐ Thirkell, Angela/MARLING HALL | | $4.95 |
| ☐ Thirkell, Angela/NORTHBRIDGE RECTORY | | $5.95 |
| ☐ Thirkell, Angela/POMFRET TOWERS | | $4.95 |
| ☐ Thirkell, Angela/WILD STRAWBERRIES | | $4.95 |
| ☐ Thompson, Earl/A GARDEN OF SAND | | $5.95 |
| ☐ Thompson, Earl/TATTOO | | $6.95 |
| ☐ West, Rebecca/THE RETURN OF THE SOLDIER | | $8.95 |
| ☐ Wharton, Williams/SCUMBLER | | $3.95 |
| ☐ Wilder, Thornton/THE EIGHTH DAY | | $4.95 |

Available from fine bookstores everywhere or use this coupon for ordering.

Carroll & Graf Publishers, Inc., 260 Fifth Avenue, N.Y., N.Y. 10001

Please send me the books I have checked above. I am enclosing $_____
(please add $1.25 per title to cover postage and handling.) Send check
or money order—no cash or C.O.D.'s please. N.Y. residents please add
8¼% sales tax.

Mr/Mrs/Ms _____

Address _____

City _____ State/Zip _____

Please allow four to six weeks for delivery.

# CARROLL & GRAF

## FINE SCIENCE FICTION AND FANTASY TITLES AVAILABLE FROM CARROLL & GRAF

- ☐ Aldiss, Brian/THE DARK LIGHT YEARS — $3.50
- ☐ Aldiss, Brian/LAST ORDERS — $3.50
- ☐ Aldiss, Brian/NON-STOP — $3.95
- ☐ Amis, Kingsley/THE ALTERATION — $3.50
- ☐ Asimov, Isaac et al/THE MAMMOTH BOOK OF CLASSIC SCIENCE FICTION (1930s) — $8.95
- ☐ Asimov, Isaac et al/THE MAMMOTH BOOK OF GOLDEN AGE SCIENCE FICTION (1940s) — $8.95
- ☐ Ballard, J.G./THE DROWNED WORLD — $3.95
- ☐ Ballard, J.G./HELLO AMERICA — $3.95
- ☐ Ballard, J.G./HIGH RISE — $3.50
- ☐ Ballard, J.G./THE TERMINAL BEACH — $3.50
- ☐ Ballard, J.G./VERMILION SANDS — $3.95
- ☐ Bingley, Margaret/SEEDS OF EVIL — $3.95
- ☐ Borges, Jorge Luis/THE BOOK OF FANTASY (Trade Paper) — $10.95
- ☐ Boucher, Anthony/THE COMPLEAT WEREWOLF — $3.95
- ☐ Burroughs, Edgar Rice/A PRINCESS OF MARS — $2.95
- ☐ Campbell, John W./THE MOON IS HELL! — $3.95
- ☐ Campbell, Ramsey/DEMONS BY DAYLIGHT — $3.95
- ☐ Dick, Philip K./CLANS OF THE ALPHANE MOON — $3.95
- ☐ Dick, Philip K./DR. BLOODMONEY — $3.95
- ☐ Dick, Philip K./THE PENULTIMATE TRUTH — $3.95
- ☐ Dick, Philip K./TIME OUT OF JOINT — $3.95
- ☐ Disch, Thomas K./CAMP CONCENTRATION — $3.95
- ☐ Disch, Thomas K./ON WINGS OF SONG — $3.95
- ☐ Hodgson, William H./THE HOUSE ON THE BORDERLAND — $3.50
- ☐ Leiber, Fritz/YOU'RE ALL ALONE — $3.95

- [ ] Leinster, Murray/THE FORGOTTEN PLANET    $3.95
- [ ] Ligotti, Thomas/SONGS OF A DEAD DREAMER $3.95
- [ ] Lovecraft, H. P. & Derleth, A./THE LURKER ON THE THRESHOLD    $3.50
- [ ] Malzberg, Barry/BEYOND APOLLO    $3.50
- [ ] Malzberg, Barry/GALAXIES    $2.95
- [ ] Moorcock, Michael/BEHOLD THE MAN    $2.95
- [ ] Cawthorne and Moorcock/FANTASY: THE 100 BEST BOOKS (Trade Paper)    $8.95
- [ ] Pringle, David/SCIENCE FICTION: THE 100 BEST NOVELS    $8.95
- [ ] Sladek, John/THE MULLER-FOKKER EFFECT    $3.95
- [ ] Sladek, John/RODERICK    $3.95
- [ ] Sladek, John/RODERICK AT RANDOM    $3.95
- [ ] Stableford, Brian/THE WALKING SHADOW    $3.95
- [ ] Stoker, Bram/THE JEWEL OF SEVEN STARS    $3.95
- [ ] Sturgeon, Theodore/THE DREAMING JEWELS    $3.95
- [ ] Sturgeon, Theodore/VENUS PLUS X    $3.95
- [ ] Sturgeon, Theodore/THE GOLDEN HELIX    $3.95
- [ ] van Vogt, A.E./COSMIC ENCOUNTER    $3.50
- [ ] Watson, Ian/CHEKHOV'S JOURNEY    $3.95
- [ ] Watson, Ian/THE EMBEDDING    $3.95
- [ ] Watson, Ian/MIRACLE VISITORS    $3.95
- [ ] Wolfe, Bernard/LIMBO    $4.95